Further praise for *The Red Car*

Named a Best Book of the Year by *Buzzfeed*,
San Francisco Chronicle, *Huffington Post*, and *Flavorwire*

"Sharp and fiery. . . . The novel's furious action keeps the pages snapping by, but each incident, at times each sentence, is bubbling with equally furious ideas. . . . There is, now, a literary term for a book you can't stop reading that makes you stop to think. It is *The Red Car*." —Daniel Handler,
New York Times Book Review

"Dermansky's writing has always been both alluring and jarring, at once intimate and detached. But with Leah, she's achieved mastery by painting a portrait of a woman who's grown out of her own life. . . . Dermansky's books are not to be missed." —Karolina Waclawiak, *BuzzFeed*

"Twisted, sexy and mysterious." —Emma Straub, *Today* Show

"A swift and magical read. . . . Dermansky's declarative language allows the reader to color in her own feelings about nostalgia, about romantic freedom, about youthful ideals and blunt wisdom. . . . Spare, funny and deftly observant of what happens when our repressed emotions reach a violent precipice."
—Maddie Crum, *Huffington Post*

"Pitch-perfect novel. . . . Sprinkled with dark humor and many literary references, Dermansky's novel is ultimately one of compassion, optimism, and fierce feminism, in which an unmoored young woman enmeshed in bad relationships with men resets her life path." —*Los Angeles Times*

"*The Red Car* is melancholy and introspective, but sharply witty and transgressive too, and it's full of the intrepid gestures I so love in fiction, both by the characters and the writing itself. There's a particular intellectual and emotional gratification to be found in this smart novel that so wonderfully blurs boundaries of reality, of past and present, of time and space. *The Red Car* is a remarkable book." —Natalie Bakopoulos, *San Francisco Chronicle*

"An erotic—and possibly haunted—journey. . . . Combining Haruki Murakami–inspired fabulism with the sexual realism of Jennifer Weiner, *The Red Car* is one of the most original novels published this year." —*Village Voice*

"Dermansky's writing is taut and smart. And it's a thrill to cheer on Leah, that admirable badass, wherever the red car takes her next." —Amy Brady, *Chicago Review of Books*

"Dry, entertaining and crookedly insightful. . . . [*The Red Car*] is on one level, a fairy tale complete with fairy godmother, and on another, a whispered goad to the reader: Live the life you really want." —Marion Winik, *Newsday*

"I've been waiting and waiting for a new book from Marcy Dermansky and finally that new book is here. *The Red Car* is taut and smart and strange and sweet and perfect. I want to eat this book or sew it to my skin or something."

—Roxane Gay, author of *Hunger* and *Difficult Women*

"Dermansky delivers a captivating novel about the pursuit of joy that combines dreamlike logic with dark humor, wry observation, and gritty feminism."

—*Kirkus Reviews*, starred review

"Marcy Dermansky's *The Red Car* is a wonder. Moving, mysterious and filled with dark, sly humor, it rustles under your skin and stays there. By the time I reached its shimmering final pages, I wanted to go right back to the beginning and start again."

—Megan Abbott, author of *You Will Know Me*

"Sleek and polished. . . . Dermansky's short, punchy chapters keep the tightly written novel moving smoothly along, and flashbacks to her past add depth without slowing momentum."

—*Publishers Weekly*

"There are few writers who can do what Marcy Dermansky does so effortlessly in *The Red Car*, the way she pushes this story in such surprising and thrilling directions, never losing control, taking your breath away line by beautiful line. Dermansky writes with such unnerving clarity about grief, not just for the loss of a loved one, but for our own unexpected lives. A strange, unflinching, utterly amazing novel."

—Kevin Wilson, author of *The Family Fang*

"[Dermansky's] latest explores the many unwise decisions of her heroine, offering no solutions but encouraging us to hope that things will get better. Readers won't be able to put this one down."　　　　　　　　—Andrea Kempf, *Library Journal*

"Don't be fooled by *The Red Car*'s brevity: it packs a serious punch. Dermansky's vision is sharp and clear, pushing her beautifully realized protagonist, Leah, into the rapids on a journey of self-discovery. And we're right there at her side, breathless, as she shakes herself awake. A tremendously moving story that feels true and important."
　　　　　—Cari Luna, author of *The Revolution of Every Day*

"Fast and unpredictable. . . . Marcy Dermansky's *The Red Car* works on us the same way Judy's car does on Leah. We are possessed to keep going, barreling toward the unknown."
　　　　　　　　　—Devan Brett Kelly, *Zyzzyva*

"A new book by the inimitable Marcy Dermansky is worth cheering for. *The Red Car* is droll, unflinching, and mysterious, a feat of efficient storytelling. I could not put it down. This novel mesmerized me."
　　　　　　　　—Edan Lepucki, author of *California*

"I've long admired the work of Marcy Dermansky, and her latest is an absolute stunner. *The Red Car* is the very rare kind of novel that—with its urgency and intrigue and deep intelligence—will pin you to your chair and transport you utterly. Stop what you're doing and read this book."
　　　　　　　—Laura van den Berg, author of *Find Me*

THE
RED CAR

THE
RED
CAR

A Novel

MARCY DERMANSKY

LIVERIGHT PUBLISHING
CORPORATION

A Division of

W. W. NORTON & COMPANY

Independent Publishers Since 1923

NEW YORK LONDON

The Red Car is a work of fiction. Names, characters, places, and incidents are the products of the author's imagination or are used fictitiously. Any resemblance to actual events, locales, or persons, living or dead, is entirely coincidental.

Copyright © 2016 by Marcy Dermansky

For information about permission to reproduce selections from this book, write to Permissions, Liveright Publishing Corporation, a division of W. W. Norton & Company, Inc., 500 Fifth Avenue, New York, NY 10110

For information about special discounts for bulk purchases, please contact W. W. Norton Special Sales at specialsales@wwnorton.com or 800-233-4830

Manufacturing by Quad Graphics Fairfield
Book design by Barbara M. Bachman
Production manager: Anna Oler

Library of Congress Cataloging-in-Publication Data

Names: Dermansky, Marcy, 1969–author.
Title: The red car / Marcy Dermansky.
Description: First edition. | New York : Liveright Publishing
   Corporation, a Division of W.W. Norton & Company, [2016]
Identifiers: LCCN 2016019280 | ISBN 9781631492334 (hardcover)
Subjects: LCSH: Self-actualization (Psychology) in women—
   Fiction. | Self-realization in women—Fiction. | Life change
   events—Fiction. | Bereavement—Fiction. | Grief—Fiction.
Classification: LCC PS3604.E7545 R43 2016 | DDC 813/.6—dc23
   LC record available at https://lccn.loc.gov/2016019280

ISBN 978-1-63149-339-3 pbk.

Liveright Publishing Corporation
500 Fifth Avenue, New York, N.Y. 10110
www.wwnorton.com

W. W. Norton & Company Ltd.
15 Carlisle Street, London W1D 3BS

1 2 3 4 5 6 7 8 9 0

For my mother,
Ann Dermansky

THE
RED CAR

I T WAS A SURPRISE TO OPEN *The New York Times* in my parents' kitchen and see a picture of Jonathan Beene. He had won an award for business innovation. They give awards like that. He was the founder of an Internet tech company that allowed individuals to fund other people's art projects, taking a small percentage of each donation. The company gave a generous share of its profits to women in the third world who wanted to start businesses. It not only supported the arts but did good in the world. Jonathan was beaming in the photo, sitting on a wooden bench in front of a small laundry somewhere in South America. He had not only just won an award. He was worth insane amounts of money.

I felt happy for him. He had been such a nerd back in college. He had proposed to me once, right before I had dropped out. It had come out offhand, in the middle of a sentence, almost like a joke, and I pretended I hadn't heard.

I stared at his picture in the newspaper.

I had not thought about him in years. Sometimes, I thought

he was a figment of my imagination. What happened between us seemed so strange. Jonathan Beene was the reason that I had dropped out of college. I had opted to leave before the school officially asked me to. Haverford was an elite Quaker college, small, proud of its honor code. On two separate occasions, I had had sex with Jonathan Beene for money. It had been an experiment on my part, a successful one I thought, until he had turned us both in to the honor board. I still cannot fathom why he felt the need to do that.

Jonathan Beene, obviously, was a much better person than I was. He had a much better life than I did, but that was easy. Most people did. I was married, unhappy, living in a small apartment in Queens. I had a job to pay the rent, but we were writers, both of us working on novels, a dream so clichéd that I was loathe to admit to anyone what I did with my days. My husband liked to listen to loud music that I did not like. Sometimes, I would go to my parents' house in New Jersey just to get away.

I had gone back to college. I took a year off and then I went back, graduating from a state school where it turned out I earned much better grades. At Haverford, I was a mediocre student, not even. At Rutgers, I did well. It was a better place for me.

HAD MADE A POINT OF losing my virginity before college. It had seemed essential, as important as doing well on my SATs. I wanted to be prepared for school.

At Haverford, however, I realized that I was at a school full of dorks and nerds and liberal do-gooders who had never done a single wrong thing. There were anorexics and overachievers, but almost no one got drunk or stoned or did anything considered vaguely unethical. My SAT scores were low compared to my classmates. I had suspected from the start that it was not the right school for me and had applied to many other colleges, artsier, funkier places, but my mother had said I would not get in to Haverford and so when I did, I went.

Jonathan Beene was the first person I met. He lived across the hall from me. He had helped me carry my suitcases into my dorm room and I knew before he had told me his name that he had a crush on me.

I had a boyfriend already. This boyfriend went to another college. He was two years older than me. He was a Republican and drove his dead father's BMW. He drove me to the beach. We had sex, all the time it felt like. I considered it practice, only sometimes enjoyable. Instructive. I had given him blow-jobs. We had gone sixty-nine. We had sex on the couch and in the backseat of his BMW and once in some bushes in the park because the idea turned him on. It was as if there was a check-list I was going down, the way most freshmen buy the things that they need for their dorm rooms. Comforter, textbooks, a new computer.

It turned out my freshman roommate had never even kissed a boy. I felt stupid, I felt so ridiculously stupid, because when I arrived, I still felt singularly unprepared. My roommate had gone to a prep school. She was fluent in French and Russian. She was bookish and pretty. She had never had a drink. I would not admit to her the things that I had done. Somehow, she liked me anyway.

I had every intention of breaking up with my boyfriend when I started college but found that when the moment came, it was difficult to do. I mean, I did break up with him, but then he started to cry. He begged me, he begged me to stay with him. He begged me.

"I love you," he said.

He had said it all summer long, my slightly older Republican boyfriend, every time we had sex, but I had just thought that he was grateful.

"Please don't break up with me," he said. "I need you."

And I didn't. Break up with him.

I took it back.

N DECEMBER, THERE WAS A DANCE. It had some sort of goofy name, not quite a formal because Haverford didn't have formals or fraternities or sororities or even a football team for that matter, but this was an actual dance and almost everyone went. My roommate went. The students at Haverford were busy catching up, all of the kids on my hall, doing all of the things that I had already done. Whereas, I didn't go the dance, because I was catching up, too. All semester long, I struggled through my classes. My freshman English teacher had told me that I needed remedial help with my writing but that he would not be able to help me because I was not a minority.

Jonathan Beene had not gone to the dance either.

He came into my room. He brought chocolate. I was trying to read a philosophy book. I was signed up for Introduction to Philosophy, and it was the hardest class I had ever taken. My eyes glazed over when I tried to do the reading. Descartes. Kant, Nietzsche. I couldn't read any of it. The texts were abstract and filled me with dread. Jonathan massaged my feet as I read. For the final, I would have to answer an essay question in which I would have to explain the viewpoint of every philosopher we had read so far that semester. Jonathan was also in this philosophy class. He loved this class. He would go on to major in philosophy. He had no problem reading these texts, and he had tried, frequently, to explain them to me without success. My brain did not compute abstract ideas. His pathetic attempt at a foot massage was annoying me.

"Do you want to have sex?" I asked.

"Leah?" he said. "What did you say?"

For my sociology class, I had read an article about teenage prostitution in Japan. They were high school students. Girls from good families who did well in school who wanted to earn extra money to buy expensive clothes. It was such a crazy idea. They would meet men in hotels, have sex and buy clothes. Apparently, this worked out fine for them. Not a big deal. Or so the girls said who were interviewed in the article. They were so beautiful, those teenage Japanese girls. They wore short pleated skirts and knee socks.

I closed my copy of *Critique of Pure Reason*.

Jonathan's hands cupped my bare feet.

"Sex," I said.

"I love you," Jonathan said. His face turned red. I felt embarrassed for him.

It seemed strange how these boys were in love with me. First my boyfriend who I had not yet broken up with, three months later, and now Jonathan Beene, who I had never even kissed.

"I will have sex with you," I said, "for one hundred dollars."

This was a surprise to me, too. I had not planned any of it. I was in a funny mood. I knew that unless I cheated on my exam, and I could easily do that, it was an open final, I would flunk my philosophy class. But I was not a cheater. I had chosen a college with an honor code. I wanted to be an honorable person. I guess I was feeling a little bleak. My roommate had gone to the dance wearing an almost new black dress my boy-friend had bought for me.

Jonathan blinked.

He did not say anything; he just stared at me to see if I was serious. We stared at each other. Suddenly his hands on my feet were not an annoyance. I felt aroused. It turned out, I was serious.

"I don't have any money on me," Jonathan said.

"There is a cash machine in the campus center," I told him.

Jonathan put on his shoes.

He was back in less than five minutes, a sheen of sweat on his forehead. He handed me five twenty-dollar bills. "This is so weird," he said.

It was weird, but I acted like it wasn't. It worked for Japanese girls. I put the money in the back pocket of my jeans. I took off my jeans. I took off my T-shirt. I was flat chested. I wasn't wearing a bra. My underwear was pink with a row of flowers on the elastic band.

"I haven't done this before," Jonathan said. His breath was shallow.

"Somehow, I knew that," I said.

It was different, being in charge. I reached my hand into Jonathan's pants and touched his erection. I watched his eyes roll to the back of his head. Though I had not expected it, I hadn't planned any of it, I felt excited, too. I pushed Jonathan back on my bed and I took off my flowered underwear. I undid his jeans. I observed his boxer shorts. My boyfriend also wore boxer shorts. I pulled Jonathan's boxer shorts down. I climbed on top of him. I was able to take him into my hand and slide him inside me. It was all very smooth, practiced. I had had practice. It was turning out to be useful, after all. I knew that after tonight I would be able to break up with my boyfriend and I felt happy about that.

"What about?" Jonathan gasped. "What about?"

"What?"

"Birth control."

Jonathan Beene was a kind and responsible boy. I had thought he might want his money back. I could picture it, that clean, crisp wad of twenty-dollar bills, folded inside my pocket.

"I am on the pill," I said.

He held onto my breasts, closed his eyes, and I did everything. It turned out I liked that better, being on top. I came for the first time that night, though I pretended not to.

ONE OF MY ROOMMATES, PHOEBE, the one who held the lease, had locked herself in her bedroom. I had not seen her in days. I would wake up for work and walk past her door. I would stand in front of it. The light was off, the drapes pulled closed, but after the rest of us left, she would turn on the lights, roam freely. I discovered this once, coming back into the apartment when I had forgotten to pack a book for the commute to work.

Every day, I would find something missing. One night I made spaghetti; when I went to drain the pasta, I discovered that the colander was missing. Alice, my other roommate, was sitting at the kitchen table eating her broccoli coleslaw without dressing. Alice was anorexic. I suppose just the fact that she was eating could be considered a triumph, but I worried that the act of eating broccoli coleslaw might actually have negative calories: that the energy expended from chewing the food burned more calories than what was consumed. I had read once that that was true for celery.

I looked at my spaghetti, floating in the pot with no way to drain it. I took a fork and started to fish out the strands of spaghetti, one by one. I didn't want to eat it anymore, not in front of Alice. I wanted to get the hell out of the apartment, buy a burrito down on Mission Street and drink a Mexican beer with a slice of lime. I wanted to go to the hip bar on Valencia Street and watch my beautiful boyfriend work the bar. He was the bartender. He was definitely a new kind of boyfriend for me. He was tall and blond and good-looking and he wanted sex, but otherwise, he did not love me, did not think it was necessary to return my calls. I was always waiting for him to call.

Slowly, I extracted my boiled spaghetti from the pot, knowing that I would not eat it. It was funny about my life. It was and it was not what I expected it to be. I worked full-time at an office. I was an executive administrative assistant for the head of Human Resources at the Facilities Management Department at the University of California. I had been stunned to get the job. My boss, Judy, said it was because I had made her laugh during the interview. I don't remember what I said that was funny. Later, she told me it wasn't anything in particular, that it was just me.

I had been an English major. For my job, I wrote descriptions of job openings for custodians and engineers and contract managers. I handled Judy's busy calendar and I took her calls. I also wrote short stories at my computer. I liked to play a video game where a geometrical worm was stuck in a maze. With every dot it ate, this worm would grow longer and longer until it crashed into one of the maze walls and then I would be dead.

"Do you want some spaghetti?" I asked Alice.

"No thanks," she said. "I already have my dinner."

I did not like having roommates. Tonight, for instance, I had the ingredients to make a sauce for my spaghetti. I liked to cook. I had olive oil and fresh tomatoes and garlic, Parmesan cheese, but I never felt comfortable cooking in front of an anorexic. It felt inappropriate. I also was not sure that I would be able to locate a saucepan. I had lost weight since moving into this apartment. That, at least, was something.

My boss, Judy, was surprised by this fact. My losing weight instead of gaining. Our relationship was not entirely professional. We told each other things. Twenty years older, Judy was always giving me advice, which, for the most part, I appreciated. Judy said that living with an anorexic would make her hungry. Judy did not suffer from feelings of guilt. She did not care what other people thought. We had had long conversations in her office about my roommates, about my love life, and also her love life, while Judy sat at her desk knitting. She had knit me an itchy green scarf that I pretended to love. I loved Judy, though I pretended not to. I had moved cross-country on a whim, far from friends and family, and often I felt unsure of myself, the space I occupied in the world.

"Why did Phoebe take the colander?" I asked Alice.

Alice shrugged. "She wants us to move out," she said.

"Well." I sat down next to Alice. My eyes focused on the joints in Alice's thin fingers. I could swear she was getting thinner. "Why doesn't she tell us?" I said. "If that's what she wants."

Alice had lived in the apartment for six years. I had been there for six months.

"She hates confrontation."

I had had so few conversations with Phoebe. The truth was I had never liked her, but I had liked the apartment, in an old

Victorian house on Castro Street, from the start. My room was tiny but I had a bay window, a view, a futon and a desk. A chair I had found on the street.

"She took the toaster," Alice said. "And the coffeepot and most of the plates."

I wondered how I had not noticed the toaster. The coffeepot had not been a problem. I mainly went out for coffee in the morning.

"So she wants us to move?"

Alice took a bite of broccoli coleslaw. She chewed very, very slowly. Then, she shrugged.

"Are you going to move?" I asked her.

"I can't afford to leave," Alice said.

"But it's her apartment."

"I have the key."

"She could bolt the door when you go out," I said.

"I know that. I am not going to go out anymore," Alice said. "I don't have a job. I just have support group and therapy. It's more important for me that I keep this apartment than go to therapy."

"What will you do when you run out of food?" I asked her.

Alice reached into her back pocket. I don't know why I felt nervous: what could this ninety-something pound woman do to me but infect me with her sadness? Any more than she already had. She handed me a twenty-dollar bill.

"You can buy me groceries," she said. "I don't need much. I am almost out of chamomile tea," she said. "And coleslaw."

I looked at the money. It would be more uncomfortable, more unpleasant for me not to take it. "I was going to ask you if you wanted to go out with me for a burrito."

Alice had done it once before. She watched me eat and sipped an iced tea. She had ordered a side of black beans and ate six beans. We went to a bookstore together where she watched me buy a book. She seemed envious, that I could buy a book. It was a used bookstore and I offered to buy her one, too. The book I bought cost four dollars. Alice had refused.

"I can't leave," Alice said now. "Phoebe might lock me out."

It was possible that she might lock me out, too, but I would take that risk.

"You want me to get you chamomile tea and broccoli cole-slaw?" I asked.

"Would you?" Alice said.

She had a look on her face.

"Anything else?"

"Some soap?"

"What kind do you want?"

"Oh anything," Alice said. "Something organic. And fragrance free."

I nodded.

"You are so sweet," Alice said.

People constantly had that idea about me. Maybe Judy was the only person who knew that I wasn't sweet. I looked at the pot on the stove, the few strands of spaghetti I had extracted from the boiling water on the plate on the kitchen counter. I would not take the time to clean up. I couldn't get out of the apartment fast enough. Chances were good Alice would clean it up for me so as not to further anger Phoebe.

"I'll be back soon," I said.

"No hurry," Alice said. "I have been out of soap for days."

HAD FOUR FAVORITE BURRITO PLACES, but I went into La Cumbre, the place I liked the least, because it was my boyfriend's favorite. On each table, there was a picture of a sexy woman with big black hair and enormous breasts that nearly escaped from her dress. She was a whore. That, at least, was what Daniel had told me. Walking through the Mission, I remembered that tonight was his night off.

Daniel was sitting at a table by himself, eating a burrito and drinking a Negra Modelo, reading Henry Miller.

"Leah," he called out to me.

He had seen me right away. I did not even have to wonder if I would have to pretend not to see him. He was happy to see me. He was so happy I wondered why he had not just called me and said, "Leah, let's go out for a burrito." But that would be too simple. I could not stop thinking of him as my boyfriend, though he wasn't actually my boyfriend, he was the poet/bartender/college dropout that I was sleeping with. He would be the first to remind me of this. The last time I had slept with him was already two weeks ago.

"I didn't come here because of you," I said, sitting down at his table. This, of course, was the same as admitting that I came there looking for him. He knew it already. Or maybe he was not that smart and would believe it was a coincidence. He looked good to me. He was wearing a black T-shirt, his blond hair slicked back.

"I love this place," Daniel said, ignoring my comment. "San Francisco is becoming so gentrified, but this place, this is the real thing. This is purity."

"Purity," I repeated.

I am not sure why, but suddenly I had a vision of Alice alone at the kitchen table. She was probably still sitting there, finishing her undressed coleslaw. I thought that her coleslaw could be considered pure.

"Tonight, I wanted a good burrito, a cold beer. I wanted a real conversation," he said. "And here you are."

You could have called me, I thought, but I did not say this. Anyway, we never had real conversations. I mainly let Daniel talk. I could not get into Henry Miller. Honestly, I thought there was too much sex in his books. I never had a good conversation with Daniel because either he did not talk at all or he never stopped talking. It was a relief to know that tonight was probably going to be a nonstop-talking night. Which meant that I was getting ahead of myself, assuming that it would be a night. That he would let me go home with him. I couldn't take him back to my apartment, not anymore.

"I haven't had dinner yet," I said. "I'm going to get a burrito."

Daniel laughed.

"Oh shit," he said. "And I thought the only reason you came here was to find me and get laid."

I looked at Daniel. I think I blushed. I did not want to blush.

"You know I am going to fuck you tonight," he said.

It was weird to me how that was exactly what I wanted,

but at the same time, I wished he wouldn't speak those words out loud.

"Okay," I said quietly.

"Let me buy your burrito," Daniel said.

"Okay," I said.

I was not sure why, but I liked it, Daniel spending money on me. It was a rare thing, though the night we met, he had bought me a drink. A vodka tonic. I was brand-new in San Francisco, right out of college, and I thought it was thrilling, a guy buying me a drink. I didn't think, how tacky, this creep is buying me a drink. I thought, how amazing, I put on lipstick and a short skirt and look what can happen.

"I am not going to get up," he said. "I am going to finish reading this scene."

He handed me twenty dollars.

I looked at the bill. I shoved it into my pocket, along with Alice's twenty-dollar bill, and I bought a burrito and a Negra Modelo. All of this money being handed over to me made me think of Jonathan Beene. I had asked him for money and he had given it to me. I did not like to think about him.

I ate the burrito and I drank the beer while Daniel read me a dirty passage of Henry Miller out loud in the taqueria. I knew, as he read to me, that someday, I would be older and that I would be mortified at myself, for allowing this to happen. I was twenty-three years old.

Part of me also thought that I should not be able to eat my burrito in front of Daniel, but I did. I was hungry. I did not like the picture of the whore on the table, but the burrito, it was good. I felt happy to be alive, to not be an anorexic, to be outside of that apartment, in a city that I loved, far from home,

from where I was from, far from New Jersey. Out of my apartment, I understood that it was a sinister situation back there.

We did go back to Daniel's apartment.

We did have sex.

I fell asleep, my head on his chest, pleased with myself, but
at some point Daniel shook me awake.

"I hope this doesn't seem weird to you," he said. "But I
would prefer it if you don't sleep here tonight."

"Really?" I said.

I started putting on my jeans before I was fully awake. I had
them on, backwards, realizing I could not zip them up that way.
Daniel tapped me on my shoulder, handing me my underwear.
I started the process all over again.

"I sleep better when I am alone," Daniel said, though this
was news to me.

"It's okay," I said. Of course, it was not okay. It was two
in the morning. I was able to find and put on the rest of my
clothes. It was safe enough to walk home. Or maybe it wasn't
safe enough, but I felt safe enough, and on the way back I
stopped into the Safeway on Market Street, which was open
twenty-four hours. I bought chamomile tea and broccoli coleslaw and even found a bar of unscented organic soap for Alice,
but when I got back to the apartment, I discovered it was locked
from the inside with the dead bolt.

Any other night, I might have thought of going to sleep at
Daniel's. Instead, I fell asleep in the hallway, using my backpack as a pillow.

JUDY SHOOK HER HEAD WHEN she saw me the next day, dressed in the same clothes I had worn to work the day before. "We used to call that the walk of shame," she said.

"I don't even know where to begin," I said.

If only I had rolled out of my boyfriend's bed.

I always felt pleased by the fact that Judy liked me. Before getting this job, I had only temped at a couple of places. I had, in fact, started out temping for her. Even before the interview, I had that going for me. I had showed her a shortcut in Microsoft Excel that she thought was clever. "You can make spreadsheets!" she said, surprised and delighted.

It was true. I had skills. I also told her about an Italian movie I had seen at an art house theater that I thought she would like. She went to see it and she liked it, too. It turned out she created the position for me. Until then, she had never had a full-time assistant because everyone bugged her too much. Judy had also tried teaching me how to knit, but it turned out that I did not have the patience for it.

I would not know until later, years later, when I didn't work for her, when I had left San Francisco, that I loved her. She looked like Liza Minnelli. She was divorced. She liked to paint. Almost everyone at the office was scared of her. She said what she thought. She had the power to hire people and also fire them. And she did fire people, frequently. Drunken custodians, incompetent receptionists, high-paid managers who went over budget. Rarely did anyone get a second chance.

I told Judy about my night, leaving out the part about sleeping on the floor of the hallway. I knew about Judy's ex-husband, an alcoholic who used to beat her before she got the hell out. She knew about my anorexic roommate and my boyfriend who was not actually my boyfriend. Still, I had to keep some things to myself. She had some clothes back from the dry cleaner, which she told me to wear.

"Really?" I said.

"You can't work looking like that," she said.

I was not only creased. My clothes were dirty. I put on Judy's black skirt, the white silk shirt, and then, the blazer.

"You look like a different person," she said.

"Bad?" I asked.

I felt uncomfortable in Judy's clothes. Like an impostor. She was six inches shorter than I was and so the skirt showed off way too much leg. Otherwise, her clothes fit.

"No," Judy said. "You look incredibly put together. I am surprised."

What this told me, of course, was that normally I did not look put together. I supposed I knew that already.

"You need a new boyfriend," Judy said.

The observation made me wince. "I know that."

"And a new place to live."

"I know that, too," I said.

Judy sighed. Sometimes she knew when to back off. Sometimes, she reminded me too much of my mother. Other times, just as irritating, she reminded me that she was boss. Now, she handed me a folder.

"Work," she said. "We have a job opening for a new admin, level three, who is going to work for Harry over in contracts. Here are some job descriptions for similar jobs for you to go on. Can you write this up for me? I need a classified ad and the job description itself."

"Okay," I said.

I reluctantly took the folder.

There were days at this job I didn't have any work to do at all. Judy liked that I worked on my fiction at the office, advised me to lie to anyone who asked me, to always say that I was working, even when I wasn't. Judy had high expectations for me. She quizzed me about my life. She always wanted me to write more, do more, be more. There were moments when I wanted to tell her to shove it. It was not like her paintings were showing in galleries, that she had a boyfriend. But I never did. At all costs, as a rule, I avoided confrontation.

"Why don't you get this done by lunch?" she said. She saw the surprise on my face. "And then we'll go out. I have something special to show you. There's a new tapas place I want to try. Does that sound good?"

"It sounds good," I said.

I could not tell her that I had hoped for a different morning. To play video games on my computer and drink coffee. She hired me to be her friend, but she also needed an assistant. The work was real. I wondered what it was that Judy wanted to show me.

I walked back to my cubicle. I noticed so many people look-ing me up and down and I wondered why. In general, I was not liked at my workplace. It was known that I was Judy's pet. The other administrative assistants knew I did not value my job. I understood this and had respect for their contempt. Many of the other employees were in their thirties and forties and even fifties. They had kids and mortgages and I did not know what else. Credit card debt.

"You look nice," Beverly called out from her cubicle as I passed by. Beverly was one of the admins in her fifties. She had long gray hair and wore oversized linen clothes to work. "What's going on? Big meeting? Job interview?"

And then, it clicked.

I was wearing Judy's clothes.

"A date after work?"

I shook my head. "I generally don't go out on dates," I said, admitting to too much.

"And that is one of the problems of your generation. All sex. No romance. No love."

I could not disagree with that.

"I spilled coffee on my shirt," I said. "Judy lent me this outfit."

Beverly nodded her head. "That explains it. The skirt is a little bit too short for an interview."

I nodded. I stood at the edge of her cubicle. It was not that I did not like Beverly. She made me nervous. She told me once that she only had fifteen more years until her pension. So she was going to keep on doing the job that she had for fifteen more years, even though she hated it. I felt like it was necessary to stay away from Beverly; I did not want her resignation to rub off on me. That was how I felt about pretty much everybody in my office. That they were all resigned to mediocrity. And who was I, after all, to want so much more? Even Judy, so high and mighty. She seemed hopelessly stuck to me.

I held up my folder.

"Work to do," I said.

Beverly gave a wry laugh. She and Judy used to be friends. They had had a falling-out. This was years ago, long before I had started working there. That was another reason I avoided Beverly, not wanting to get in the middle. But really, it was because Beverly was preparing herself for death, and while I was not entirely satisfied with the circumstances of my existence, I felt like the possibility of improvement still existed. That I could make happiness happen. That night, for instance, I was determined not to sleep on the hallway floor.

To get to my cubicle, I passed four more cubicles, and then Diego's office. Diego, he was different from the rest. He was also young, only a couple of years older than me. He wore slick suits, crisp shirts, silver and navy blue ties. He had a degree in architecture from a good school. He was from Costa Rica. I had an enormous crush on Diego. We were friends. He was clearly not interested in me and so it helped when we out for lunch or hung out by the water cooler that he knew that I had a boyfriend.

"Leah," he called out. "You look so nice today."

It was an invitation. I came into his office, sat on his desk. It was a flirtatious move on my part. That was what we did. Besides lunch with Judy, flirting with Diego was my favorite part of the job.

"You should dress like that more often," he said.

"They are Judy's clothes."

"Let's go out for lunch today," he said.

I shook my head. "Can't," I said. "I am having lunch with Judy."

"That's cool."

"We are going out for tapas."

"Totally cool."

It was revelatory, really. If I dressed differently, the hot guy in the office would ask me out, even if it was only for lunch. Who knows? I might even get ahead, succeed, earn more money. That, of course, wasn't what I wanted. My position at the office wasn't temporary, but I continued to think of it that way. I wondered if I could cancel on Judy and then go out for tapas with Diego instead.

"Work to do," Diego said.

I slid off his desk, brandishing my folder.

"Me, too," I said, and I did.

The funny thing about doing work at my job was that I was good at it. I was able to blend three old job descriptions from other positions into a new one for Judy. I knocked off the ad to post on the HR website, another one for the newspaper, and coded all of the entries properly with ID numbers, the proper codes and HTML tags. I knew that Judy would be pleased with my work. She would review, approve, make one unnecessary change just to prove her superior position, and then the job would be posted.

Judy was smart and Judy had hired me. She had seen something in me. Even if I didn't want to get ahead in the field of human resources. The job actually paid well. I had enough money to rent my own apartment, buy my own furniture. No more crazy roommates. But I was afraid to do it, afraid that renting an apartment meant that I was forever compromised. Whereas Judy said what it would mean was I had a nice apartment and nothing more. Judy often had smart things to say to me. Most of the time, I didn't listen to her.

She was not surprised when I showed up at her office at noon and handed her the completed work.

"Thanks, doll," she said, giving it a cursory glance. "I knew you would get this done."

Going out to lunch with Judy was usually expensive, but Judy was my boss, and most of the time, if it was just the two of us, she paid, putting the tab on the office account. We walked to the parking lot together. I felt myself growing excited. A new restaurant. A long lunch.

"Look," Judy said, squeezing my hand.

"What?" I said, surprised but also pleased by the physical display of affection, not usual for Judy.

I looked and what I saw was the parking lot. I saw parked cars. I looked for Judy's car and I did not see it. I followed Judy's extended arm, not sure what I was looking for. My gaze traveled from her arm down to her red nail polish to a blindingly red car, gleaming in the sunlight. A sports car. I blinked. I felt as if I had gotten something in my eye.

"It that yours?" I asked.

"I have always wanted a car just like this," she said. "Come see. Can you believe it? It's a dream come true."

I wasn't convinced. It was a car. Who dreamed about owning a red car?

Judy had once told me she wanted to go to Hawaii. She told me she wanted to paint large canvasses. A mural. This, this was just a car. I wasn't sure why, but I knew that I didn't like it. It was a feeling I had. I shivered.

"It drives like a dream, too," Judy said.

There was that word, again. Dream.

A bad dream, I thought.

I thought about spending the night on the floor in front of my apartment. I hadn't had any dreams. Strangely, I had slept well. I followed Judy to her new car. She unlocked the car with a loud beep from her key chain and I got in.

"I didn't know you wanted a red car," I said. I felt almost betrayed, that she hadn't told me.

"All my life," Judy said.

I touched the smooth leather of the upholstery. I put on my seat belt. I checked to see if the seat belt was secure. The car was too low to the ground. It had new car smell, something chemical and cloying, and I opened the window even though it was cold outside. "I feel like something sinister has happened in this car," I said. "Or could happen. I don't know. Something bad."

"I don't know what you are going on about," Judy said, her voice sharp. I hated it when Judy was displeased with me. "But save it for one of your short stories. This car is all good. It's brand-new. It is perfection."

I looked away, stung, not sure if Judy was putting down my short stories. But that wasn't it. I had responded wrong. A gesture had been required and I had let her down. It was Judy who was disappointed.

I hated that I had disappointed her.

I had disappointed my mother, moving so far away after college. By not calling home. By keeping secrets. I did not want to be a disappointment.

"Congratulations," I said. "Don't listen to me. What do I know? I take the bus. This car. It's beautiful. Look at this leather interior. It's so soft, Judy."

The leather, it *was* soft. I did like it. I looked at Judy, her short dark hair, her red lipstick. I saw how pleased she was, with her car and even with me, once again, pleased with the compliment I had paid her new car.

"You are beautiful," I said, meaning it.

I had never thought that before, about Judy. Because she was small and she looked like Liza Minnelli. But she was, beautiful.

Judy smiled at me, placated.

"This is the nicest thing I have ever bought for myself," she said.

"That's nice," I said.

Judy started the engine. It was loud. Too loud. My feelings for the car, despite what I had said, had not changed.

"This is it for me," she said. "This car."

"That's not true."

"You're just a baby," Judy said. She put the car into reverse. "I forget that sometimes."

"No," I said, offended. "I am not."

But I had never had tapas before. She drove us to the restaurant she had picked out. I was distracted. I realized I was not sure what I would do, after work, what I could expect. If I had a home to go back to. I let Judy order. The car had upset me. Judy had found a parking space right in front of the restaurant and I could see the red car from our table. Taunting me. There was something about the way she talked, too, that

reminded me of Beverly. Of fifteen more years at the office. A
life sentence. I wanted Judy to return the car. To quit her powerful job. But she would never do these things. This, as she had
said, was it for her. I was not a baby. Somehow, I felt older.
Like I had aged in a day. Judy ordered a carafe of sangria. The
waiter asked to see my ID.

The sangria was delicious.

"I have high hopes for you," Judy said, refilling our glasses.
"You know that. You are going to do incredible things."

"No," I said, though I wanted to. "I am not."

"I am going to make sure of it," she said.

"No," I said.

"Let's celebrate."

"Celebrate what?" I asked.

"The day," Judy said. "This lunch. My red car. To our
future good fortune."

The waiter came to our table with a tray full of small plates
of food. Judy had ordered well. Fried potatoes, roasted arti-
choke hearts, sautéed mushrooms, calamari.

We made a toast.

"This is the best calamari I have ever had," Judy said.

I smiled at Judy. It was also the best calamari I had ever
had, though I couldn't say how many times I had had calamari.
Three, maybe. Perhaps four. I was not a baby, but I had more
to do. I felt content again in the moment, with the food, with
her company. I didn't even mind the red car if it made Judy
happy. It was not my car, after all. It was not my life. We were
both a little bit drunk by the end of the meal.

"I can't drive like this," she said, laughing.

We drank one espresso and then another.

We sat at our table in the window, unable or unwilling to leave. "Screw the office," she said.

I laughed, delighted to hear these words come out of my boss's mouth. I think I knew even then, that afternoon, when we never ended up going back to the office, that this day was something special. The waiter brought us an order of caramel flan, on the house. We shared the dessert, taking small bites with small silver spoons.

"Delicious," Judy said, smiling at me.

TEN YEARS LATER

I T WAS BEVERLY, FROM THE OFFICE, who wrote to tell me that Judy had died. It had been a car accident. Another car had gone through a red light and plowed directly into Judy's red car, no longer new, and she had died, instantly. Her neck had broken on impact. I read the email from my apartment in Queens as my husband cooked dinner.

I was not sure how to process the information. Judy was dead. We had lost track of each other over the years. She had been happy for me when I quit my job to go to graduate school. I had been her assistant for two years and I had begun to do my work slower and then slower still. It was Judy who had urged me to apply to writing programs. She even proofread my short stories, locating typos and offering praise that I didn't deserve. Once I got in, Judy threatened to fire me if I didn't go.

Still, it had seemed ridiculous at the time: to leave a good-paying office job to get a degree in creative writing. Creative writing. Judy, for instance, had a graduate degree in painting and look where that had gotten her. To a higher-paying office job.

Beverly's email was a shock.

I had woken up early that day, before the sun had come up, and snuck out of bed, gone to my desk that was also the kitchen table and cleared space for my computer. I had written the last scene of my novel. It had come as a surprise to me. I had not realized I was so close. I had finished my novel. The entire day passed and I had not told anyone. I had not told my husband, Hans. Always looking for a reason to celebrate, he would have run out to buy a bottle of champagne. I had written the last sentence and I felt a humming inside me, a sort of quiet happiness. I did not want to ruin it.

Judy was dead.

I sometimes thought I applied to graduate school to avoid renting my own apartment. To get away from Daniel who I had actually lived with for an entire year. From the start it was understood that it was temporary, he was low on cash, and when he asked me to leave, I sublet a room for a couple of months in the Haight, and then another room out by the ocean, and then I left. I went down south, to a writing program in Louisiana, of all places, where I had received a fellowship.

The dead bolt on Phoebe's apartment on Castro Street never opened. I came home from work and found my belongings in the hall outside the front door: my laptop computer, my cheap desk, some but not all of my clothes neatly folded in my suitcase, which had once been in the closet. Phoebe had forgotten my stuff in the bathroom, I remember, which was annoying to me. I had new bottles of Aveda shampoo and conditioner. It's funny how I remembered that shampoo still because I no longer bought myself Aveda products. They were out of my price range.

Judy had bought me a leather backpack, a going-away present. My boyfriend who was not my boyfriend had told me he loved me.

"You are kidding me," I said.

But he wasn't. He had become less beautiful to me in the year that we had lived together.

"You are telling me this now."

"I didn't know until now," he said.

Instead, not long before I left, I made out with Diego, but he wouldn't have sex with me.

"I don't have sex with drunk girls," he said.

That made no sense whatsoever to me. There was no way, in any capacity, that I would have had the courage to make a pass at Diego if I weren't drunk. Also, I was leaving. At least he did kiss me. He did put both of his hands around my ass and leave them there. "You are funny, Leah Kaplan," he said. "I am going to miss you."

I thought about all of these people, people from my past life, my life in San Francisco, they all flashed before my eyes as I read and reread the email from Beverly about Judy. I thought about Alice and her broccoli coleslaw. I did not know what had happened to her. For all I knew, she was also dead. I felt tears well in my eyes. I wanted to call Alice. I did not have her phone number. I could not even remember her last name.

At the end of the email, Beverly asked me to call.

Hans watched me from the kitchen, stir-frying the shrimp.

"My boss died," I told him.

Hans and I had been married for five years. We had met in graduate school and had left Louisiana together for New York City because he had always dreamed of living there. Hans was from Austria. He was in the kitchen, making pad thai. He was very proud of his pad thai. He bought noodles at the Asian market and fish sauce, limes, bean sprouts and peanuts, and fresh shrimp, tofu. It was a production. Whenever he made it, it was my job to tell him how good it was. And it was good, but it wasn't any better than the pad thai that came from the local Thai restaurant and didn't require profuse praise and sometimes sex afterward.

"Scottie?" he asked. "Holy shit."

"Oh," I said. "No. Sorry. Scottie is fine. Still an asshole." Well, that wasn't fair. Scottie wasn't an asshole, but he paid me by the hour, and for a while, I had been doing my work too quickly and therefore not being paid enough, but I had figured it out and I had slowed down. "Judy," I said. "Judy died."

I had told Hans about Judy, at least I had thought that I had, but the name was not familiar to him. Scottie was my current boss. It was not a crazy surprise that after completing my MFA, I had gone back into administrative work. At first I temped, and then I had gotten hired full-time by the place where I temped, and then when the economy crashed, I had gotten fired from that same job. Not long after, like the best birthday present ever, I was rehired, a part-time gig working from home. It was perfect, the perfect job for me. I was lucky. I knew that I was lucky. Whenever I was impatient with my life, I told myself that I was lucky.

Judy had died.

She was dead on impact, a broken neck. I thought of her shiny black hair, her head bent over at the wheel. I had never felt safe in her car. I had not been in contact with her for a long time, three or four years, but I did not want her to be dead.

Hans left his pad thai on the stove to wrap me in his arms, but I did not want to be held and I squirmed out of his embrace.

"It's too hot," I said.

It actually was. It was a hot summer.

Judy had warned me about getting married. I had written her to tell her that I was getting married to my boyfriend from graduate school but I was slightly apprehensive. His student visa was about to expire and if I did not marry him, he would have to leave the country, go back to Europe. I loved him and I did not want him to leave. It felt as if I had no choice. It was not a good feeling.

"You might not want to hear this," she wrote, "but I am going to say it anyway. Don't get married if you are not sure. Even if you love him. Marriage changes everything. It sucks you in and leaves you dry. Don't do it if you are not sure. Don't do it because of a green card."

I didn't take her advice. It was exactly what I wanted to hear and it also wasn't. I had already agreed to get married. I imagined how hurt and angry Hans would be if I told him I'd changed my mind. I couldn't fathom it. Hans, my sweet goofball Hans, had an ugly temper. He had once thrown a plant during an argument about something I could no longer remember, breaking the ceramic pot when it smashed against the floor. Later we walked to the hardware store together and bought a new one, replanted the small plant together. I had discovered that I liked having plants, though I did not take the best care of them. I had a tall ficus. A potted African violet on the kitchen windowsill.

And why would I listen to her? My old boss. Her life was no

example. She had married an alcoholic. She worked in Human Resources in a Facilities Management Department. Painting for her was just a hobby. I did not want to be a hobbyist. I wanted to be the real thing, a writer. So I pulled away from her after that email. Which was easy enough. She lived across the country.

Judy had died.

She was dead.

I was thirty-three years old and I did not have much experience with death. I knew in theory that I had to prepare myself for certain things. My mother would die. My father would die. But none of my friends had ever died. No one I had ever been close to. I had lived a blessed life and I didn't even know it. I went back to my computer and did a quick search of my email. My last email to Judy had been three years ago. I told her that work was going well on my novel. I told her about a trip I had taken to Belize with Hans and the beautiful fish we had seen snorkeling. I had been bragging. I had felt like it was necessary for her to know that I was happy.

"She was the short one, right?" Hans said. "Who drove the red car?"

"She got killed in her car."

"That is awful," Hans said. "Baby."

He began clearing the coffee table in front of the TV in the living room. He brought out two beers, beer mugs from Austria, and the pad thai. He began looking for the remote control for the television, which was always, invariably lost. I watched him do all of these things and did not offer to help. "What do you want to watch?" he asked.

I am not sure how it started. Probably, because we did

not have a dining room table, we always ate on the couch, and most of the time, we watched a show or a movie while we ate. Like me, Hans was working on a novel. But he also wrote reviews for the entertainment section of a website and so we were always getting DVD screeners. He made a small amount of money writing these reviews, but basically it was my part-time job that paid our rent. We were always broke. I bought cheap shampoo.

"I don't think I'm hungry," I said.

"But I made pad thai."

"I know you did. I'm sorry."

I sat down at my computer and read the email again. Beverly wrote that I should call. "I'm going to make a phone call," I told Hans. I picked at an old pimple on my chin, reopening a scab.

"Don't do that," Hans said. "You are ruining your face."

I had started picking at my face after I had gotten married. Not a lot, just when my skin broke out, which it did, without fail, once a month, as if I were still a teenager.

"I am going to make this call in the bedroom."

"What about dinner?"

I looked at Hans. He was like a puppy. Why did he want so much praise for making dinner? In the refrigerator, I had a bag of broccoli coleslaw. It was something I had learned from Alice. It was the easiest way to make sure that I ate cruciferous vegetables, though I did not have mine plain. I mixed my coleslaw with mayonnaise and lemon juice. I would have happily had coleslaw and a beer. Or melted cheese on a tortilla. Or a chocolate pudding and a beer. I would have happily not eaten dinner at all.

That was something I had discovered once I married Hans.

Every night, he wanted to eat dinner. He wanted to know what I wanted for dinner. He wanted to know who was going to shop for dinner. He wanted to know what we wanted to watch when eating dinner.

"You can start without me," I said. "I don't feel hungry."

"I bought the large shrimp," Hans said.

I stared at him. "My friend died," I said.

"I thought she was your boss."

I shook my head, my arms hanging down at my sides. She was my friend and I had loved her. I was an idiot. I was such a fool. Sometimes, still, I heard her voice in my head. I would be swimming laps, and I would think, today, maybe I will write Judy, and then, I didn't. I went into the bedroom and closed the door. I sat on the bed. It felt strange to call Beverly. I remembered my last day of work. They had a send-off party for me in the office and I felt guilty because I felt so overwhelmingly giddy to be leaving, and they were all staying. That was the night I made a pass at Diego. I did the math. Ten years had gone by. Beverly had five more years until retirement. I supposed, really, that that was not very long.

"

AM SORRY TO TELL YOU the bad news," Beverly
said.

"I am sorry you have the job of telling me bad news."

"Do you remember?" Beverly said. "I never thought Judy
should have bought that car. I told her that."

"The car made Judy happy."

I sat down on the edge of the unmade bed. I tried to remember. Did I make the bed that morning? Yes, yes I had. At some
point in the day, Hans must have taken a nap. He had not
remade the bed. These were the things about being married
that I hadn't anticipated. Judy knew. Judy had warned me.
Judy had never met Hans.

I got up and pulled the comforter straight. It took a couple
of seconds. I walked over to the window and I opened it. It was
surreal, looking out into the small fenced-in backyard. We did
not have access to the backyard; it belonged to the landlord and
his family who lived downstairs. This summer they had put in
a tiny aboveground pool that completely filled the space. Outside, the two Morillo kids splashed in the water. I felt a fresh
tear roll down my face.

"She named me the executor of her estate," Beverly said.
"She left you the car. And some other things."

This took me by surprise. The car was Judy's most precious possession. Also, she had died in that car. A car crash.

"It's not totaled?"

"Apparently, it's not," Beverly said. "It's at a mechanic's. He is waiting on you for how to proceed."

"How to proceed."

I felt a little bit dumb. It was a Thursday and it was hot outside, ninety something degrees. Could that explain it? I could hear Hans's TV in the living room. He was watching something with shooting in it. Guns and police sirens.

"I don't want the car," I said.

"I think you should respect Judy's wishes."

"I don't think she wanted for me to have a wrecked car. It's crazy that she left me her car. She loved her car. It was her most prized possession." It looked nice, the Morillo's swimming pool. It was small, but big enough that I could have floated on my back, looked up at the sky. "You said there were other things."

"She left you a small painting and a sealed envelope. I have it here at the office. I don't know what is in the envelope. You need to come out here, sweetheart."

A painting. An envelope. A red car. I bit my lip. It was cruel of the Morillos to put in that pool. Cruel to taunt me like that. I thought about jumping out the window, jumping into their swimming pool, how surprised they would be. But it wasn't feasible. Yes, I could jump out the window, but there was no way to take a running start. Probably I would land on the small strip of concrete just in front of the pool. I would jump out the window and I would break some bones.

"I think you should come," Beverly repeated. "The funeral is tomorrow. I should have called you sooner. I did not know about the will."

"You are kidding me," I said. "I can't come to a funeral tomorrow."

I wiped the tears from my cheeks. Lately, I felt like I couldn't do anything, even though Hans constantly told me otherwise.

"I checked online, sweetheart, and there are flights. They are expensive, granted, but there are flights."

"I can't come," I said.

I wasn't sure why I insisted I couldn't come. I wasn't sure what plans I had for the next day. I had work, but I could get out of work. Anyway, it was a telecommuting job. I could do my job in California. I had ideas for how I was going to spend the day. There was a movie I wanted to see. Or maybe I was going to go to the Russian gym I belonged to around the corner and swim laps. Suddenly, I remembered the novel I had finished that morning. I had finished it. I had finished my novel. Maybe I was going to go sit in a café and read my novel. That was something I wanted to do.

"Give me the phone," I heard someone say, and then Diego was on the line.

"What is your problem, Leah?"

"Diego," I said. Suddenly, I was grinning. Clutching the phone, the biggest smile on my face. "You still work there?"

"Yes, Leah, I still work here. Don't be rude. I am a manager now. Do you have a problem with that?"

"Do you have a girlfriend?" I asked.

"In the plural," Diego said and he laughed. I remembered

that laugh. He was so good-looking. Latin. Why was it that I had married an Austrian? Hans was so methodical about things, while at the same time, he was such a mess.

"Get yourself on a plane," Diego said. "This is Judy we are talking about."

"I loved Judy," I said.

"I know you did. She knew you did."

"We haven't talked in years," I said. "I think I hurt her feelings. I used to write her emails in my head, but I never sent them."

"It doesn't matter."

"It does matter."

"I had lunch with her last week, Leah," Diego said. "It doesn't matter. We talked about you."

"You did? You talked about me?" I did not know why I was so hurt. Why hadn't they called me? Judy. Diego. Why was Judy dead? There were no tissues in the room, just an empty tissue box. I wiped the tears from my face with the bottom of my T-shirt.

"Are you crying?" Diego asked.

I shook my head. "No," I said. It was obvious that I was crying. "I'm not."

"Do you know what I am doing right now?" he said.

I shook my head again, knowing that Diego couldn't see me. I did not know what he was doing.

"I am putting a work order into the computer."

"A work order," I said.

"Done," he said.

"That was fast," I said.

"I type faster than anyone."

I remembered. He had long, slender fingers.

"Okay," Diego said. "So I found a flight that leaves in four hours. It's the last plane out tonight. You get into San Francisco insanely early, more like the middle of the night. You'll be in time for the funeral. I will be heroic and pick you up at the airport. Can you do that?"

I shook my head. "No," I said.

"Why?"

"I'm married."

"So?"

I did not have an answer to that.

"Do you have a baby?" Diego asked.

I shook my head again.

"Are you pregnant?"

"No," I practically screamed.

"Well, your husband can take of himself."

"He made pad thai for dinner."

Diego missed a beat. He did not know quite how to respond to that. "Well, good," Diego said. "When do you want to come back?"

"Come back?" I asked.

"I thought you went to writing school."

"I did," I said. "Why?"

"Well, your articulation of the English language is lacking. When do you want to come back? Your return ticket. I have to put something into the computer."

"I don't know."

"Does a week sound good?"

"No," I said, surprising myself.

"It doesn't?"

"I don't think it's enough," I said.

"I think you are right," Diego said.

"I could go to Calistoga," I said.

"Wine country," Diego laughed. "Mud baths."

I had gone to Calistoga, once, with Daniel. We rode there on his motorcycle, stayed in a bed-and-breakfast, swam in an outdoor Olympic-size pool filled with sulfur water from a natural spring. California, it seemed like a dream.

"Do you know how Judy died?" I asked.

"It was a car accident," Diego said. "Didn't Beverly tell you?"

"But how? Can you tell me again? Because I don't understand."

I remember sitting in that car, Judy driving me home once late at night, after we went to a movie, I remember feeling like there was something else in there, with us. I remember thinking that death was inside the car, hovering close by.

"Another car plowed right into her. Apparently it sailed through a red light. Completely not her fault."

"That is so awful," I said.

"Done," Diego said.

"What?"

"I just booked your ticket. You fly back in two weeks."

"Two weeks." I didn't know. Was that long enough? Too long? Two weeks in San Francisco. I was supposed to be unhappy, but the idea of it made me happy. "How much does it cost?"

"No worries." Diego laughed again. I loved his laugh. It was so loose and sexy and easy, just like Diego. "The department is paying for it."

I could hear noises, splashing out the window, the TV in the living room, the buzzing in my brain.

"What am I going to tell Hans?" I said.

"Hans?"

"My husband."

"You tell him you are going to the funeral of a dear friend and then on a small vacation. I have no doubt you deserve one."

I was not entirely sure why, but I felt afraid. The idea of telling Hans. I did not want to tell him. I wondered if I could ask Diego to tell him for me. That was ridiculous.

"Your flight leaves in four hours, Leah," Diego said. "You have the money to take a cab to the airport, don't you?"

"Of course, I do," I said, though actually I didn't. I would have to run to the corner to a cash machine.

"So start packing."

"I can't believe she is dead," I said. "Judy."

"I know," he said. "It doesn't feel real. I'll pick you up at the airport."

"You will?" I asked. "Really?"

"I'll see you tomorrow," Diego said. "I got to go. I'll see you tomorrow."

"Can I talk to Beverly?" I asked.

"Nah," Diego said. "Beverly wandered off somewhere. She is probably at the water cooler, complaining about how much more work she has to do now that Judy is dead."

I laughed. That was probably exactly what she was doing.

"I am sending you an email with the confirmation of your ticket," he said. "Airline, flight number. I'll see you soon."

DIDN'T WANT TO TELL HANS that I was going to San Francisco without him. But now that the ticket was bought, I felt giddy. Giddy and a little bit confused. How could I be happy when Judy was dead? Judy had not wanted me to get married. And now, now that she was dead, I was leaving my husband. Only, I wasn't leaving him. I was just taking a trip. That was all that I was doing.

It was good that I was already in the bedroom, the door closed. I opened the closet door and took out a small suitcase, put it on the bed. I packed ten pairs of clean underwear. Socks. Jeans. I took off the jeans I was wearing and put them in the suitcase, too. I did not want to fly in jeans. I would wear leggings. Hans knocked on the door but came in without waiting for me to answer.

"What is taking so long?" he asked.

"Get out," I said. "I am getting dressed."

Hans looked confused. "We are married," he said.

I didn't like the way he was looking at me. I had taken my jeans off. I was wearing striped cotton underwear. Of course, he would have ideas. Hans always wanted to have sex with me. I mean, that made sense, we were married. Some people would say that was a good thing, but I almost never wanted to have sex. It was fine, sex, when we had it. I just never wanted to. I hastily picked up a pair of gray leggings off the floor and put them on before he could get closer to me. I felt that even though we were married, I was entitled to my privacy. He had knocked on the door. He could have waited until I said, "Come in."

"That was a long phone call," he said. "I have been waiting for you."

"I'm sorry," I said. "I told you not to wait."

"I wanted to wait," he said. "I made us dinner. I want to eat it with you."

Somehow, Hans hadn't noticed the suitcase, so I left the bedroom. I wasn't sure what I thought I would do, maybe pack in secret and climb out the window. I would have to tell him. I didn't know what my problem was, why I was afraid. Our friends thought he was the nicest, kindest man in the world. But none of them ever got to see him angry, that was all reserved for me. And I knew my going to San Francisco, that would get him angry. He would want to come. I was sure that he would want to come. Diego had only bought one plane ticket.

I walked slowly over to the couch in the living room. There, on the coffee table, were the two untouched plates of pad thai, the beer mugs, one half full, an open beer, Sriracha hot sauce.

I would not be able to eat this food.

"Judy's funeral is tomorrow," I said.

"Oh," Hans said. "That is sad."

It felt to me as if Hans had already forgotten that she had died. He wanted us to eat dinner, watch the next episode of *Six Feet Under*. Hans had never met Judy. I had never told him that Judy had told me to put off getting married. Probably, I had told him very little about her. She didn't really figure into my life anymore.

"I guess I am going to her funeral," I said.

"What do you mean?"

"I have a plane ticket and I am going."

"How can you have a plane ticket?"

"I don't know. It happened so quickly. Diego filled out a work order and used the company credit card and I have a plane ticket so I can go to her funeral tomorrow."

"Okay," Hans said. "I want to come, too."

I blinked. I knew him, I knew him too well. Sometimes, Hans would say that we shared a brain and what one of us didn't know about ourselves, the other knew. I never thought of this as a good thing. I wanted full possession of my brain.

"I am going for a funeral," I said. "Judy left me some things in her will. I have to go. You never even met her."

Hans stared at me. He was growing his hair long again, even though I preferred it short. The pad thai sat untouched on the coffee table in the living room.

"I have been telling you for a while now," Hans said. "That we need to go on a vacation."

"This isn't a vacation," I said quietly.

"How long are you going for?" Hans asked.

The answer, I knew, was wrong.

"Two weeks," I said, even more quietly.

"Two weeks?"

"Diego bought the ticket."

"Who is Diego?"

"This guy I used to work with. He is in management now.

Actually, I'm not sure. That's what he said. I just know he used company money to buy me a ticket."

"Well, great, call him back and tell him you want him to by me a ticket, too."

"I can't do that."

"Why not?"

"I can't."

"We are married. Married people go to funerals together. This is common knowledge."

"You didn't know her."

I had told him that. I was having difficulty breathing. It had been a while since our last fight. I hated fighting with Hans. I hated fighting. I hated it.

"We are married."

"I am sorry," I said. "Diego bought the ticket. He got the only available dates." This part, it wasn't entirely true, but it sounded good. "I can do my job from the West Coast, it won't be a problem."

"But what about me?"

I looked at Hans.

"I want to go, too," he said.

"The plane ticket is in my name," I said.

"Not alone. I want to go with you. I want to go to San Francisco. With you."

I shook my head. I had tried to tell Diego that Hans would react this way.

"You'll be fine," I said, remembering what Diego had said. "Look at how well you cook. You can take care of yourself for a while."

Hans threw his pad thai across the room, breaking the

white plate, noodles flying everywhere, small bits of chopped peanuts landing on the white wall, bean sprouts on the floor.

"Call him and ask him to get me a ticket, too."

"It's a funeral," I said softly.

"It's not just a funeral. You are going for two weeks."

"You'll be fine," I said, my eyes focused on a single bean sprout on the floor. "You are a grown man. I would love it if you were to go away for two weeks." I knew that I should stop talking but I could not stop talking. "I would do anything to be alone for two weeks. I am grateful when you go out for the night."

It happened so fast I didn't even see it coming. I don't know how it happened, Hans's hands were around my throat and he was choking me, my legs were twisted out from under me, and I was on the floor, unable to breathe.

I wet my pants.

Hans stopped choking me.

I lay there on the floor in my wet leggings and didn't move. Hans lay next to me. I don't think he saw it coming either. Nothing like that had ever happened before. Now, he was stroking my hair.

"Oh, Leah," he said. "Leah. I am so sorry."

I think I nodded.

We both lay on the floor, breathing hard.

"I am just going on a trip," I said. "Can I go on a trip? Please."

"I am sorry," Hans said, again and then again. "I don't know what happened. I don't want to be alone. I don't want you to go. I want to go with you."

"It's just a short trip," I said.

"I don't want to be left all by myself. Please don't go."

"It is just a short trip," I whispered.

And maybe that had been true.

Before Hans choked me.

N THE AIRPORT, I WAS SURPRISED by how little it took to make me feel happy again. I bought an *Interview* magazine which featured a French actress that I loved being interviewed by an American actress that I loved. They were both starring in the same movie directed by a Polish director whose movies I also loved. I bought a bag of Peanut M&Ms. I bought myself a coffee. I sat at the gate, reading my magazine and eating my M&Ms, drinking my coffee.

I watched the people at the gate who would also be boarding my flight to San Francisco. I saw a family, a mother with two babies, and I wondered if I would ever be her. I had never talked to Hans about whether or not we wanted to have kids. I watched a businessman look very serious and important, typing important things into his laptop. I had also packed my laptop computer. I could sit at a table and type fast, appear to be a very important writer. I could wear my thick tortoiseshell glasses, the ones that made me look more like a writer.

It seemed incomprehensible that just a few hours ago, Hans had choked me because I was going to go the funeral of my old boss who was dead. And that not long before that, we had been about to eat dinner and watch a new episode of our favorite TV show. It seemed incomprehensible that I was off to spend two weeks in San Francisco. I could not remember what I had packed.

I did not know what I should be more upset about. That Judy was dead. That Hans had choked me. That I did not feel in control of my life. How every day happened, and then the next day, and I didn't have a greater plan. I remembered, again, that I had finished a draft of my novel. That I did have a plan. It seemed as unreal as Hans choking me. I had been thinking I might tell him my news while we were eating pad thai. This was before I had gotten the email. Instead I found myself cleaning pad thai off the hardwood floor. It was something to do, while waiting for the cab to the airport.

I decided to shut off my thoughts like I would shut my laptop computer. Click. I would give all of my attention to the French actress. I learned that she had been in a near death accident while waterskiing and had to have emergency brain surgery, but now she appeared to be perfectly fine. In the interview, she talked about her new film, the accident, her famous father and also her new album, because not only was she an actress, she had a music career beginning to take off. I had her new album. Hans had gotten it for me without my asking because he knew that I wanted it.

Hans, he could be thoughtful. He loved me.

An amplified voice called out that boarding would begin, first class and disabled passengers, passengers with children. I watched the line starting to form. I looked at my boarding pass to check my seat number. I was in row 8. That seemed like a very low number. I went to the counter. The woman looked at my ticket and told me that my ticket was first class. I could board now.

"I am not first class," I said.

The woman smiled at me. "It can sometimes be considered a state of mind," she said. "But your ticket is first class, so you can board the plane."

She looked at the magazine that I was clutching to my chest. "I love her," she said, pointing to the French actress on the cover of the magazine.

"So do I."

"Cool," the stewardess said, but then I remembered that the word was no longer "stewardess," and that it was possible that she would not actually be on my flight. This was unfortunate, as I wanted her to be my friend. I wanted her to sit next to me on the flight and we could talk about French movies and I could tell her that my husband had tried to choke me when I had told him about my trip, but that that was an aberration, and that he was a very sweet man, and that in the past, more than one person had proclaimed to envy me because I had married such a sweet man.

I boarded the plane.

Row 8 was the last row in first class.

"Look at all this legroom," I said.

Suddenly I could sense the presence of Judy, my dead boss, nodding in approval. This surprised me. I was not one to see ghosts and I did not think Judy was the type to be a ghost. She was much too practical for that.

I wondered if Diego knew that he was buying me a first class ticket. He must have. He must love that his job allowed him to do things like that. He was a manager. I had always thought that he would go back to Costa Rica and become a diplomat. I had never thought he would still be at the office.

I had forgotten about Diego. I felt excited to see him. I buckled my seat belt.

After the flight took off, I drank my complimentary glass of champagne and then I asked for another. I did not eat the meal that was offered to me, though it looked good. The idea of dinner made me think of the one that I had not eaten. The idea of dinner made me feel guilty. I wanted to turn off my thoughts. Click. I asked for and received a third glass of complimentary champagne.

"Not too much," I heard Judy tell me, but she didn't mean I shouldn't drink that particular glass already in my hand. She meant that I simply should not drink another. And so I didn't. I drank my third glass of champagne and then I accepted the soft pillow the stewardess gave me, not the nice woman from the gate who I had hoped would be my friend, but another kind woman, and I could not remember what it was we were supposed to call them now. Cabin attendant maybe, though that was dumb, there had to be a better job title than that, which reminded me that I used to write job titles when I worked for Judy who was dead.

I wish that she hadn't died. I wished that I was going to visit San Francisco, and, at some point during my trip, I would go back to the office, and I could go out for a boozy lunch with Judy and Diego. In this imaginary lunch, they would both tell me that they envied me for pursuing my dreams while they still hadn't gotten out of the office. I would tell them about my novel and they would make a toast to me. Judy would show me her new painting, it would be hanging on the restaurant wall, and I would tell her that I loved it. I would love her painting. Under the table, Diego would tickle my knee.

"I am a little bit drunk," I told the cabin attendant. She also looked nice. She was a black woman whose head was closely shaved. She was beautiful and I wished that she would be my friend, too.

"Perfectly okay," she said. "As long as you don't raise your voice or make unreasonable demands."

"I won't," I said. "I promise."

"I am not worried," she said. She handed me a soft blue blanket.

"This is such a nice blanket," I said. I rubbed the blanket to my face.

"Maybe you should go to sleep," my cabin attendant said, and I realized I didn't want her to be my friend. I wanted her to be my mother. I had not yet told my mother that I was on a flight to San Francisco. It had all happened so quickly and I had not thought to call her. I had not invited her to my wedding. It had been a civil service at City Hall. I hoped that the plane would not crash. I could imagine my mother, who watched the news every night while eating dinner and then again before going to bed. She would watch the story about the plane crash and she would feel horrible, thinking about the friends and family of everyone who had died, the thought never occurring to her that I had also died. Somehow, the shock of it, when they announced the passenger list, would make it worse.

The beautiful cabin attendant knelt down at my seat and pressed a button. "Tell me when to stop," she said as I went from vertical to horizontal.

"Go all the way," I murmured.

My seat had turned into a bed. It felt more comfortable than my bed at home. The cabin attendant smoothed the blanket over me and rearranged my pillow.

"Is this how you treat everyone in first class?" I asked. My eyes were closed. I had this wish, for the black woman with the close-shaved head to kiss me on my forehead and wish me good night. I don't think she did, but I felt something. I felt a kiss on my forehead. It wasn't real, but it also was. Maybe it was from Hans, but I didn't think so. He had called the taxi that had seen me off, even gone to the ATM himself to take money out from our joint account so that I could pay for the taxi, and then apologized again and again. But I knew that deep down he was still mad at me for leaving. The kiss could have come from my mother, but I didn't think so. She was watching the news or maybe she was walking the dog.

Still, my eyes closed, almost asleep, I knew that someone had kissed my forehead, had wished me a good night's sleep.

Diego, maybe.

Or Judy, who was dead.

How I wished she hadn't died.

DIEGO PICKED ME UP AT the airport.

He wrapped me in his arms. He kissed me on the lips. He was wearing a black suit and was almost ten years older than the last time I saw him, but he still looked like a boy to me.

"Leah," he said.

I realized that the kiss wasn't a kiss, like a real kiss, because this was different. This was about death, about grief.

"You shouldn't always believe the things you tell yourself," Judy said.

Judy, there she was again. Talking to me. I did not understand it. I could hear the timbre of her voice, the inflection, but, of course, no one else could hear her. And I didn't actually believe that she was actually talking to me. For years, when I started graduate school, and then, when I moved to New York, I could hear Judy talking to me, giving me advice, taking note of my decisions and offering her approval. Her disapproval. But it stopped once I had gotten married. I gradually stopped sending her emails and I could not hear her voice. She was gone. The stupid thing was that it was not until after I learned that she had died that I realized that I missed her.

"Pretty stupid," Judy observed.

"Do you have anything to wear to the funeral?" Diego asked me.

I shook my head.

I had forgotten to pack funeral clothes.

I did have breakfast in the airport, waiting for Diego, so at least that was taken care of.

"We have time to go shopping," he said.

I very much did not want to go shopping, but I didn't want to disagree with Diego, because he knew more about certain things than I did, and he also looked like a male model, especially in his suit, and I wanted to look good, too, so that he would not be ashamed of me.

"Did you check a bag?" he asked.

I shook my head. I had only my knapsack and a small carry-on.

"Good." Diego approved. "We have more time."

Diego drove us to Macy's on Union Square. He used valet parking and he took us directly to a special counter where he told a salesgirl that I needed a black dress. "She needs to wear it a funeral, today," he said. "So there is no time for alterations. The dress should also be nice," he added. "For a party."

"I know just the thing," the salesgirl said, eyeing me up and down.

We sat down in the velvet armchairs in the lounge of the dressing room and we waited. This did not approximate any experience I had ever had shopping before.

"What's wrong?" Diego asked.

"How can you tell?"

Diego shrugged. "Something about how you are sitting. Your shoulders look funny."

I sat up straight.

"I told Hans I would call him when we got in, let him know I arrived safely."

"He would find out if you hadn't," Diego said, reminding me of my mother. "It would be on the news."

I nodded. Still, I had told Hans I would call him. It was 2001, a new millennium. Cell phones were no longer new. Still, I did not have one.

"I promised," I said.

Diego reached into the pocket of his black suit and gave me his cell phone. "Call him," he said, and I was grateful, even though I did not want to talk to Hans. I had barely been away, but I had promised that I would.

He answered on the first ring.

"It's me," I said.

"Hi, you," he said.

There was a silence.

"I had an amazing flight," I told him. "I flew first class and I slept through the entire trip."

I had been disappointed when I woke up to find out that we were ready to land. I felt like I had missed out.

"I was worried," Hans said. "I miss you."

"I miss you, too," I said, looking at Diego who was almost studiously not watching me. The salesgirl entered the dressing room, holding a stack of black dresses.

"I have to go," I said. "I am trying on dresses for the funeral."

"Did you say you flew first class?"

"Let's start with this dress," the salesgirl said.

I stood up to look at it, snapping the cell phone shut. I realized that I had not said good-bye to Hans. I could call him again, say, "Sorry, I forgot to say good-bye," but that seemed even worse than what I had just done, which I realized was not good, so I turned my attention back to the salesgirl and the dress she was holding.

I loved it right away. It was sleeveless, simple, something Audrey Hepburn would have worn in *Breakfast at Tiffany's*.

I took the dress behind the curtain and tried it on. It fit. I did not look at myself in the mirror because I had a problem with looking at myself in the mirror, but I knew that the dress was expensive and beautiful, and so there was a possibility that I looked beautiful, too.

I could not reach the back zipper.

I stepped out of the changing room.

"That is perfect," Diego said. Without my asking, he stepped forward and zipped me up.

"I have the perfect sweater to go with it," the salesgirl said.

She disappeared and then reappeared with a wraparound black sweater, which she draped over my shoulders. It had black floral edging. We would be going from Macy's straight to the funeral.

"Good," Diego said, rubbing his hands together. "You look beautiful. Could we cut the tags off?"

I had to step out of my dress for the salesgirl to remove the tags to my new dress, which I did, and then I paid for my outfit. I had wondered if Diego would pay for my clothes or if perhaps the office would, but as that did not seem forthcoming, I gave the helpful woman my credit card.

I felt different riding the escalator out of Macy's, stepping into Diego's expensive car, buckling my seat belt. I felt like an alternate version of myself and this was the person I would be at Judy's funeral.

IEGO DROVE TO MARIN.

We didn't talk. I was happy about this.

I looked out the window as we drove over the Golden Gate Bridge, thinking about Hans waking up in our apartment without me, making a pot of French press coffee, using too much coffee, and later pouring the grinds into the sink and then not rinsing the sink, and then I turned off the thought and I looked at the water beneath me. I loved it here. I had walked across the Golden Gate Bridge, but only once. Maybe I could do it again. I didn't know. It was a possibility.

Judy's service was held in a small red barn. I had not thought about it, not until now, but I realized how special it was that Judy even had a funeral at all. Her family was all on the East Coast, from a suburb outside of Philadelphia. She had an older sister she used to talk about bitterly, and elderly parents that she used to mock, telling me about her less than pleasant yearly visits back home. If her parents were still alive, they would be too old to fly. So if her family was there and her service was here, I wondered who would mourn for her. I wondered if I had a right to mourn Judy.

"This is a lovely spot," I said.

The barn looked like something Judy would want to paint. It was right on the water.

"She left instructions," Diego said. "For the funeral. She set aside money for it. She had been painting here for years. Beverly did everything."

"I thought they had a falling-out," I whispered. I did not know why I was whispering. I tried to remember the last funeral I went to. It had been for Hans's ninety-year-old grandmother in Austria. She had been a schoolteacher in a one room school during the war. Before her death, the family had grown exasperated with her. She had become notorious for repeating the same stories about the war, telling them over and over, as if always for the first time. I wished that I could have listened to these stories but she only spoke German. The service had been in German.

"On again, off again," Diego said. "These older single ladies. They are like cats. They were friends when she died."

I felt slightly offended by this comment but I didn't respond. There were three rows of benches, filled with people I both knew and did not know. Judy's paintings hung in the barn. She painted flowers and cats. Which is not to minimize the quality of her work. I loved flowers and cats and her work was actually quite good. Beverly had said she had left me a painting and I wondered which one it would be.

Beverly was already there, wearing a flowered dress and Mary Janes. She came over to me and gave me a warm hug. I had literally not given her a single thought over the years and there she was.

"So sad" is what she said and I nodded my head in agreement.

I said hello to other people from the office; two building managers, men in suits whose names I could not remember, the Englishwoman who took the calls at the customer service

desk, her name was Hailey, and Ruby, the receptionist at the
front desk who had never liked me. There was a cluster of
older women who I guessed were from Judy's painting class.
There was a guy in his fifties wearing a leather jacket and
wire-rimmed glasses. He had a goatee. Maybe a boyfriend.
Occasionally Judy had them. He also could have been another
painter.

I felt like I did not belong there.

I wobbled in my shoes.

"How does this work?" I whispered to Diego, who, for
reasons I did not understand but was grateful for, stayed close
to me.

"I hate funerals," he said.

I nodded, because this made sense to me. I had only been to
two. There had been Hans's grandmother, an affair that had
been completely without meaning. Afterward we had gone to a
traditional restaurant where I ate spaetzle and drank too much
beer. I also had an aunt who died of leukemia when I was thirteen, and that funeral was completely surreal. Her boyfriend
at the time was an epileptic alcoholic from Copenhagen and
at one point during the reception, he went off to throw up in
the bushes. I could not bear to look at my cousins, because it
seemed too awful, losing their mother, and I had never gotten
along with them. They had grown up in the country and did
not do well in school.

It occurred to me again that I had so little experience with
death. Thinking that was a horrible thought, a little bit like
Jinx, because now that I had thought it, perhaps I had willed
someone I knew to die. My mother, my father. Diego. I took
Diego's hand. I wondered if we would have sex.

"You might," I heard Judy say, but Judy was dead.

It was weird how she had started talking to me. Unnerving. Where had she been, all these years? Why had she allowed me to drift away? We were at her funeral and I was married and Diego did not want to have sex with me. He had made that clear a long time ago. I was not allowed to have thoughts about having sex with Diego. I was married. I had been choked by my husband. Did that change the rules? I wondered what Judy thought about that. Nothing. She thought nothing about that. But I was at her funeral and perhaps I was not supposed to be thinking critical thoughts.

Beverly stood up at the front of the barn and the room quieted. "We are here to say good-bye to our dear friend Judy," she began.

I was crying. It was ridiculous. It was embarrassing. I hoped that Judy would not be mad at me.

FOUND MYSELF THINKING ABOUT DOLPHINS during the service. How beautiful they were. Sometimes, on the weekends when I was in graduate school in Louisiana, I would drive my car to Biloxi, Mississippi, where I would take a boat to Ship Island. It was a short ferry ride, which I loved. You almost always saw dolphins in the water, swimming alongside the ship. There were dolphins in the water in the Gulf of Mexico. I had not known that before I went to school there.

I would go to Ship Island by myself and I would swim. Even from the beach, you could see dolphins, leaping from the water and their gentle return back into the sea. It was a magical place.

I remembered writing Judy an email about Ship Island, about going there by myself, the sun on my face, the dolphins. How I loved it there.

The crazy thing about Ship Island was that it no longer existed, not the way that I remembered it. There were a series of hurricanes and, at least for a short period of time, the island had been swallowed up by the sea. I read that repairs had been made, the visitors facility rebuilt. It was a place where I had been happy, but I would never go back again. That part of my life was over.

AFTER THE FUNERAL, JUDY'S ECLECTIC group of friends and co-workers went to a nearby Mexican restaurant for lunch. Diego ordered a pitcher of margaritas. I licked the salt on the edge of my glass. I drank my drink too quickly. I liked the salt. I felt sad about the dolphins. Melancholy. I felt floating unexplainable melancholy. Loss.

Beverly took my hand.

"After lunch," she said. "We'll go see the car."

I had forgotten already. Judy had left me her car in the will. I hadn't driven in years, not since moving to New York. Really, the only time I had ever driven was when I was in graduate school when the supermarket was three miles away and the mall was four, and driving was absolutely essential.

"I don't want the car," I said. "Judy died in it."

Diego poured me another margarita.

The man with the leather jacket and the wire-rim glasses came up to me and shook my hand. "She told me all about you," he said.

"Who?" I said.

Okay, I was drunk already. There had been actual lunch at the restaurant, tacos and guacamole, and somehow all I had been able to do was drink. I picked up a chip and I dipped it in the guacamole and I ate it. It was good, so good. I didn't know who this man was but somehow, he knew who I was.

"I haven't seen her in years," I said.

He shrugged. "That doesn't change a thing," he said. "Love is what it is and she loved you." I wanted to ask him who he was, but he said that he had to leave.

"Guy is an asshole," Beverly whispered to me. "He totally played with Judy's heart."

"He spent her money, too," Diego added.

"A boyfriend," I said.

"I wouldn't call him that," Beverly said.

But it was something. If not love, maybe sex. Someone. At least Judy had gotten laid. I didn't like the idea of Judy dying alone.

"But I did die alone," Judy said, matter-of-fact. "I was alone in my car. Though I guess you could also say that I was with my car. I loved my car."

But then, I wanted to argue with Judy, everyone dies alone. You can't die with another person, or even if you do, like in an earthquake or a car accident or a fire, or in a hospital bed with a lover holding your hand, your actual death is still a solitary thing. Why did I want to pick a fight about this in the first place, when I wanted to believe that Judy hadn't been alone? Of course she was. It occurred to me that I did not know a thing, which made me wonder why I thought I could be a writer. It was time to leave the restaurant. I ate some more guacamole.

Beverly told me that lunch was over. The funeral was over. The busboy began to clear the table. Diego was holding my hand. "Thank you," I said.

I had two more weeks in San Francisco.

We drove back into San Francisco to see the car. Diego dropped me off at the garage. Beverly had forgotten her promise to take me.

"Aren't you coming in with me?"

"I have work to do, sweetheart," he said. "It's a workday."

I don't know what I had thought. That he would take care of me, not leave my side. I did not even know where I was sleeping that night. I did not like how he called me "sweetheart." I felt dismissed by the word.

"Drive back to the office when you are done here and meet me," he said. Which was a little bit better. But somehow not actually better.

"Won't the car be undrivable?"

"Then take a taxi."

"I could take the bus."

"Don't take the bus," Diego said. "You're overdressed."

I nodded, unsure. Maybe Diego had fulfilled his obligation to me. Or to Judy. I was married. I was not supposed to allow my feelings to be so easily hurt.

"Can't you stay?" I asked him.

Diego shook his head ruefully. "Judy died the week quarterly reports are due. I have to put in a budget. I might have to work late tonight. I don't know yet."

My carry-on bag was still in the trunk of his car. I decided not to say anything. Even if Diego and I hadn't talked about it, I would sleep at his apartment tonight. Where else would I go? It was what I wanted to do.

I could almost see Judy nodding. Oh, how I missed her. Now. Now, I missed her. Now.

"That is the whole point," she said. "About being on this earth. Doing what you want to do. That is what I did. Also, you are right. You can be an idiot. I forgive you."

I T TURNED OUT WHAT JUDY had wanted to do was die. She had left a letter for me to find in her car.

THE MECHANIC SEEMED PLEASED TO see me. I did not have to introduce myself.

"You the owner of the red car?"

I nodded and followed him from the office to the back of the garage.

"How did you know?"

"They told me you were coming today."

That, then, was not much of a mystery.

I blinked when I saw Judy's car. I felt the margaritas turn in my stomach and I wondered if I would throw up. I could taste the bile in the back of my throat, as if I had caught the vomit and pushed it back down. There I was, face-to-face with Judy's red car. The entire left side was smashed in, the face of the car that had killed her imprinted in the metal.

Oh, how I knew that smashed-in car. We had driven over the hills of San Francisco. This car had taken me to so many lunches, dropped me off on the rare days that I had worked late. Taken me to Marin and Sonoma, and once, a weekend in Mendocino. I had never liked this car. As a passenger, I had always felt much too low to the ground. Unsafe. Jostled. Bumped over every bump. I had never gotten past the new car smell. But I had never told Judy this, because she loved her car.

"You can't fix it, can you?" I asked the mechanic. I wanted the answer to be no.

"Sure, I could," the mechanic said. "It's just bodywork. A lot of bodywork."

The mechanic had a long beard; he wore a Grateful Dead T-shirt. This reminded me of my husband, who had a short beard and owned a handful of Grateful Dead T-shirts. I averted my eyes from the skeleton on the mechanic's T-shirt.

"Won't it cost a lot?"

"Insurance is going to cover it."

"Won't it cost as much as the car is worth?" I asked.

"Just about," the mechanic said. "But like this, sweetheart, the car is worth nothing. I fix it, you have a red car and I get a lot of money."

"Okay," I said. I did not know why everyone was calling me sweetheart.

"Okay?"

"Okay, fix it, I guess," I said.

I had learned lessons about the value of money from my father. When I was still a child, he had explained to me over Chinese food that all wars were fought over money. I had argued passionately about the Civil War, about the emancipation of the slaves, and he had told me that slaves were worth good money, like an expensive horse or an automobile, and that the war was all about money. Nothing else. I remember the disappointment I felt. It was a lesson I did not want to learn. But, now, in the auto body shop, I was not going to throw away good money. I was not in any kind of position to do that. I would have the car repaired. I would sell it. Hans was writing a novel, too. We had to pay rent. I looked at the car. Judy's car.

"Can I sit in it?" I asked. "Just for a second?"

He nodded. I took a seat in the passenger side, my seat. I buckled my seat belt. I remembered the last place Judy and I had gone to lunch before I left for graduate school, a touristy restaurant right on the ocean, the Cliff House, because I told Judy I had never gone there.

"That is ridiculous," she said. "They have terrific French onion soup."

We took a three-hour lunch that day. We had French onion soup and gin and tonics, took a walk along the beach. I rolled up my pants and put my feet in the water. Judy said it was too cold. She shook her head fondly at me.

"I will miss you," I said.

But I hadn't.

Or I did, but only for a short while. It wasn't as if she was my mother. Or a friend my own age. She was my boss, she had been my boss, and so it did not make sense to stay in touch. Not when what she had to say no longer pleased me. I had fit her neatly into a category that did not quite apply. Who else did I go for walks with along the beach, get along with like that? There was no one. There was no one else.

"I am sorry," I told Judy now, sitting in her car.

She didn't answer.

I would have liked if she had answered.

I put my hand under the seat, I don't know why, and I found an old journal of mine. It was a Japanese notebook with a navy blue cover, skinny lines, filled until the second-to-last page with my illegible scrawl. I remembered how bereft I had felt when I lost that particular journal. I had looked everywhere for that book, torn up my apartment, gone into every café and bar I frequented and asked if I had left it there. Now, I held it to my chest. Had it sat under the seat for years and years? Did Judy know that it was there? This had been the book I had written in, questioning my feelings for Daniel. My guilt about Alice, wasting away in front of me. Where I wondered, do I go to graduate school? Do I rent an apartment and live like a grown-up? What do I eat for breakfast? I opened it to a random page and closed it.

I was not sure, actually, that I wanted to read these pages. I wrote journal pages just to write them, never to revisit. Taped to the back cover was a sealed envelope, my name written on it with a black calligraphy pen. I recognized Judy's handwriting.

Judy had written me a letter.

She had written me a letter.

I could suddenly feel it, like a wave. Judy had died in this car. What was I doing, breathing that air? I struggled with the door handle, unable to get out quickly enough.

"Don't fix the car," I told the mechanic.

The mechanic looked at me.

"What about the money?"

I blinked. I did not understand the question.

"I will fix the car and then I'll sell it for you," he said. "And I will give you the cash. We can work out the details. Okay?"

"Okay," I said, changing my mind again, quick as that. I did not feel any less panicked, but that did not matter. My father would be pleased with me. But I would not get back into Judy's car. I was glad that was settled.

The mechanic took my hand and led me back to his office. I sat down on the plastic chair across from his desk and was not surprised when he brought me a glass of water. It was easy to make fun of the hippies, but often they were kind. I knew, for instance, that when he sold the car, he would give me the money.

"He might not," Judy said. "I wouldn't trust him."

Judy had a less favorable opinion of hippies.

"Judy, my friend, she died in that car," I told him, both hands on my water glass, afraid that I might drop it. "I don't think anyone should drive it."

"You are probably right," he said. "How about I sell it to a creep?"

This made me smile.

"She wrote me a letter," I said.

I showed him the envelope.

"Your dead friend," he said, gently. "You gonna read it?"

"Not here," I said.

"Are you going to give me your phone number?"

I looked at him.

"So I can call you after I fix the car."

I nodded, dumbly. I wished that I had a cell phone. I gave him my home number, the one I shared with Hans. And then I wrote down my email.

"It would be better if you emailed me. I share that number with my husband. Back in New York."

"You don't wear a wedding ring."

I shrugged. I wondered if the mechanic was going to ask me on a date. There was nothing that I would like less. "It was uncomfortable," I said. "When I did yoga."

This was true, though it had been a long time since I had taken a yoga class. I found it difficult to relax during a yoga class. My mind raced during the slow parts, I could not begin to do a headstand and I was always watching women more beautiful than I was, stretching more deeply than me. And while I had these inappropriate competitive thoughts during a nonjudgmental yoga class, I judged myself for my thoughts. Of course, I stopped going. I had also never liked wearing my wedding ring. We had bought matching gold bands at a discount jewelry store on Route 17 the day of the wedding. It was uncomfortable during yoga, uncomfortable when I slept. I worried about losing it when I swam in the ocean.

"You wanna get high?" the mechanic asked.

I tilted my head to the side.

"You look." The mechanic paused, as if searching for words. "You look as if you need something."

"No," I said. "Not really."

The mechanic seemed to be waiting for something more.

"I don't want to get high," I said.

THE LETTER FROM JUDY

Leah,

*If you are reading this letter, it means that I am
most likely dead and you have found your journal
under the seat of my car. I have held on to your journal for all these years, sometimes rereading it. It was
difficult for me to read, you should know. Your handwriting is such a fucking mess, but I suspect that is
on purpose. You are hiding from yourself as much as
you are hiding from everyone else. Wearing clothing
several sizes too large. Dating men who are not worthy of you. Men who are either indifferent to you or
smother you with their love.*

*I have never met a person so in need while also
so unaware of how needy she is. I think that is why I
hired you. And smart. Also, I liked you right away.*

*It broke my heart when you left to go to graduate
school, even though I was glad to see you go. I helped*

push you out the door, didn't I? I knew it would be good for you.

I know you will be a great writer. I know things, you don't always believe me, but there are some things I know. You think leaving was all your idea, but I had threatened to fire you, hadn't I? You never worked very hard, and after you left, my new assistant did a much better job. I never took her to lunch. We were not friends. I had learned my lesson.

I loved you, Leah, though I don't think you appreciated me. Because I was your boss and not your mother. Because you did not respect me for having an office job. You had this idea that your life would be so much more than mine. You never liked my red car. I am not stupid. I don't think you thought that I was stupid. I don't think you valued me enough.

Here I am, writing you a letter to read when I am dead, believing that my words will mean something to you. It seems odd to me, choosing you, when I don't believe you valued me enough. Shouldn't there be someone else? Well, let me tell you: it is hard to find true love. Or just love. To love and be loved back. Also, you were young, you did not know better. You are still young. I have been lonely. I made peace with my loneliness long ago. It is hard to be five foot one and wear thick glasses and meet a man worthy of my wit and intelligence. All my life, I have been underestimated because of my height.

My first husband was a drunk. He threw me down

*a flight of stairs and he said it was an accident and
maybe it was an accident, but I still broke my arm.*

*To tell you the truth, Leah, I also thought that my
life would be so much more. I am not that old, only
fifty-three, and I have enough money in the bank that
there is no reason for me to kill myself now when I
can buy a plane ticket instead and go to Hawaii. I
know that if I were in the Pacific Ocean, swimming
with sea turtles, something you wrote to me about
once in an email, my outlook about life might be very
different. I might not want to die. I could go to Italy
and drink red wine and eat pasta and not give a damn
about the calories. I might still want to die, but at
least I would have had a good time before I go.*

*I can't explain it. Why I won't go on a last vaca-
tion. I don't think my life would turn into a Diane
Lane movie. I don't want to waste the time.*

*I have taken to driving recklessly, closing my eyes
while driving on a highway—just for a second at a
time. Speeding through yellow lights.*

*I am leaving you my car, which I think you also
underestimated, and also some money. I am also hoping that you will figure out, now that I am dead, that
you actually did love me. Though we haven't emailed
in a while, too long, I know you need money. Because
you chose to be an artist. Because you married someone you probably shouldn't have.*

*If I leave Leah money, I think to myself, she can
leave her husband. Presumptuous, right? I know my
advice to you was one of the reasons why you stopped*

*talking to me—and I have always regretted that.
Because I miss you. But it was also impossible for me
to not tell you how I feel. I am sorry I read your journal. Or maybe, Leah, you left it in my car for me to
read it.*

*Do what you want, Leah. It might seem hard to
believe me, seeing that I am dead, but I have lived the
way I wanted to. I would even say that I was happy.*

*One more thing. One last thing. I recently received
an invitation to my niece's bat mitzvah. My sister
and I have not spoken in a long time. Perhaps I will
be able to go. I bought a plane ticket and reserved
a hotel room. Not Hawaii, not Tuscany, but Penn-
sylvania. I don't believe I will be here, on this earth,
on the day of the event, and therefore will be unable
to attend. I would appreciate, if that is the case, if
you would go in my stead. I have not seen my niece
in many years. I dislike my sister, we haven't gotten
along, not since we were kids, but it occurs to me
that most likely my niece is a perfectly wonderful
girl. Perhaps she needed a hip older aunt like me to
save her. I suppose that is my one regret. Go tell her
that. Would you do that for me?*

*I knew when I bought that car that I might die in
it. I have really never loved anything as much as that
red car.*

xox,
Judy

THE AUTO BODY SHOP WAS located in an industrial district. There was not a taxi to be caught. I did not have a cell phone to call Diego. I did not want to ask the mechanic for any more help, because I knew how that would go. He would be kind to me, let me use the telephone, and I would somehow feel like I owed him. I would go out to dinner with him, or coffee, or out to hear a band, and then have to tell him no, again, and sometimes, if I didn't feel like saying no, I wouldn't. Which was almost never a good idea: the random one-night stands in my life. Not that I would ever have sex with the mechanic. I just did not want to ask him to use the telephone.

Though it occurred to me now that men had stopped hitting on me, as if I had become invisible once I got married. Until I bought this black dress.

"No," Judy said. "It's the vibe you have been giving off."

"The vibe?" I asked. "What vibe?"

"It's not good. Almost toxic. Your body language says stay away."

I changed my mind. I did not like having Judy's voice in my head. She was dead. It was my choice to allow her to haunt me. Was it my choice? I could not predict what she would say. When she would say it. Nothing she said was comforting or easy.

And there was another voice in my head, also nagging me, that I wasn't listening to at all, Hans, who I knew was getting progressively angrier at me for not calling. Even though I had already called once. That morning. I had hung up on him. Shit. He would want to hear from me again. I had not had a chance to call. I could have asked the mechanic to use his phone, but that occurred to me only now, as I walked aimlessly in what I was pretty sure was the right direction toward I did not know what. I couldn't even get myself to ask the mechanic to call me a taxi, let alone make a personal call. I walked past a bus stop just as a bus pulled to a stop, and so I got on it, not entirely sure which direction it was going.

"The Castro," the driver said.

I didn't have a bus card.

"You can't buy them on the bus," the driver said.

I blinked.

"I just came from a funeral," I said.

I realized that might not have made any sense, given the neighborhood I was in, but I was wearing a black dress.

"Just have a seat," the driver said.

I moved back quickly, so as not to attract any attention, taking a seat in the back row. Muni. I was remembering how it worked: my Fast Pass, a monthly bus card instead of a Metro-Card. I used to buy mine at the small market across the street. What else? What else had I forgotten about living in San Francisco? The views, always sneaking up on me, the bookstores, Golden Gate Park, the sea lions at Pier 39. The ocean. The burritos. Italian food in North Beach.

But I had left. I had left because I was stuck. I had left because after two years of working for Judy, I was afraid I was too comfortable at my job and would never go anywhere, do anything. I left because I had this boyfriend who never seemed to care when I broke up with him, but was always happy when I came back. I left to get away from all of those things. I left to be a writer. I left to get a graduate degree.

I had one of those now. A degree in writing. I had a possessive husband. We had had that fight, but I wondered if it was real. I had not told anyone. Not even Judy, or the ghost of Judy, knew. And so, maybe, it had not happened. Or was not as bad as I thought it was. I had a new job, one where I did not have to work from an office. Soon, I would have to get to my computer and do that job: picking news stories that went on to corporate websites and rewriting the headlines. Judy's funeral conveniently fell on my day off. Tomorrow, I told myself, I would make sure to do my work.

"Good girl," Judy said.

It was strange how alive she felt, now that she was dead.

"You are forgetting something," she said.

"What?"

I looked out the window of the bus, going up and down the hills, the view of palm trees in Mission Delores, and then I remembered. I remembered that I had written a novel.

"That," Judy said.

I wasn't sure. I would have to reread it. For now, I rode the bus to the last stop. The bus, of course, was not an accident. I was meant to catch that bus because it turned out that I knew exactly where I was going. The bus let me off at a stop only blocks away from my old apartment on Castro Street, and so I walked there. From the street, I would be able to look up at my bay window, my pretty small room on the third floor, where I spent those crazy few months when I lived with Phoebe and Alice.

The clothes I had worn on the plane were in my backpack, so in a matter of seconds I could go back to being me. Was that what I wanted? I could walk down to a taqueria and change my clothes in the bathroom. I could eat a burrito, go to a used bookstore, a café. It was like I was taking a tour of my old life, as if maybe the old me had died, too.

I looked up at my window.

I had loved that little room. I had loved my desk. I had loved my laptop computer, the first one I had ever bought. I had felt like my life was full of promise. It was a shock when I found out that Phoebe was bat-shit crazy, that Alice was starving herself to death. It took all the pleasure out of my small and inexpensive room. I wondered, again, if Alice was still alive.

I very much hoped that she was.

Someone came down the steps of the apartment, an attractive gay woman. Or maybe that was a wrong assumption for me to make. But she looked gay and the Castro was a neighborhood full of gay people. But then, I had lived there, too. It was not required for residency. Still, of course, this woman was a lesbian. Her hair was short. She was wearing a tank top and khaki cut-off shorts. She had tattoos on her arm. Her arms were muscled. She looked strong. Suddenly, I felt shy. I liked the way she looked, more than my fancy Diego-approved clothes.

"It's okay," Judy said. "You look lovely."

I was getting irritated with Judy, always contradicting me, even when she was being kind, and I didn't believe it was her anyway, it was my own fucking head, fucking with me. So really, I was getting irritated with myself.

"Can I help you?" the beautiful woman with the short hair asked me.

"I used to live here," I said.

"No shit?"

"Yeah," I said. I pointed to my room on the third floor. "The bay window. It had a dreamy view."

"That's my room."

"Really?" I said.

"The closet was full of stuff," she said. "When I moved in."

"Stuff?"

"Yeah," she said. "Clothes. A nice blanket. Notebooks full of writing. A desk."

"That could be my stuff," I said.

"You want to check it out?" she said.

"Could I?"

"I was just going to a café to do some writing."

I named the name of my favorite café.

"Yeah, that was a good one. That place went out of business a couple of years ago but there is another place not far from here."

I stood with my hands at my sides, sad about my favorite café.

"Do you want to see if the things are yours?"

"It was ten years ago," I said.

"Stranger things have happened."

"Do you have the lease or do you rent your room from someone?"

"A woman named Phoebe," she said.

"You're kidding me."

"She's a real recluse."

I laughed. "She might not want to see me."

"Same Phoebe?"

I nodded.

"I had a feeling about her when I moved in," my new friend said. "But the deal was so good. Right on Castro."

"I think she takes in roommates when she runs out of cash."

She turned around and I followed her into my old building, which was pretty much the same except the peeling gray paint on the wall was peeling more than before, coming off in sheets. I pulled down a strip with my hand and then realized what I was doing and stopped myself.

"I like your dress," she said, as I followed her into her bedroom, which had once been my bedroom. I had to remind myself that we were not actually friends. "It reminds me of Audrey Hepburn."

"I went to a funeral today," I said.

"I'm sorry," she said. "Someone you were close to?"

"Yes," I said.

I wondered what Judy would have to say about that. She did not comment.

The woman whose room it now was went to the closet and she pulled out three cardboard boxes. "I keep meaning to give the clothes and books to charity, but never get around to it. I guess this is why."

I sat down on her futon. I was loath to look at my things. There, I saw on top of the pile, was what was once my favorite cardigan. I used to wear it much too often. It was a shapeless garment. I did not want to wear it ever again. I could still hear the words from Judy's letter in my head. Her comment about my oversized clothes. I didn't know what it all meant. Her car had been hit, plowed into, and yet what I read had felt like a suicide note.

My new friend sat down next to me. She took my hand. Her hand was soft. There was dirt under her fingernails. There was dirt under my fingernails, too, even though I was wearing a pretty dress.

"I have never been to the funeral of a person I cared about before," I said.

A tear dripped down my cheek. I wasn't crying for Judy. I did not know why I was crying. She saw the tear; she wiped it away with her finger. She leaned over and kissed me. I had never kissed a woman before. I had always wanted to kiss a woman, but had never had the opportunity. Actually, that was not true. In college, a friend had made a pass at me and I had turned her down. I had been too nervous to respond properly. I wondered, sometimes, whether my life would be different if I had kissed her back. Maybe we would have fallen in love. I would have moved to Somerville with her, another gay neighborhood, this one outside of Boston. I might have liked that. I would have never married Hans.

My new friend had soft lips. She tasted good, like coffee, even though she had told me that she was on her way to a café.

"You taste good," I said. "Like coffee."

"You taste like tequila," she said, laughing.

"We went out for drinks after the funeral."

I kissed her again. I somehow could not help myself. I had not asked her her name. She had not asked for mine. Arms around each other, we lay back on her futon. It was so nice, just kissing and touching, her hands in my long hair, my hands on her head, the soft buzz of her scalp. She unzipped my expensive black dress and I slid myself out of it. Her hands were on my back, running over my breasts, up and down my legs, in between my legs. I could not believe I was actually doing this. This was so unlike my experience of sex with Hans. I felt like I was enjoying myself too much. I was enjoying myself too much and this made me feel guilty. I sat up.

"Too fast?" she asked.

I nodded.

"You are not gay?" she asked.

I nodded again.

"I hate that," she said. "Straight girls."

"I liked the kissing," I said.

The woman kissed me again. She also gently probed her finger inside me, this time underneath my underwear. Who was to say that I wasn't gay? I was thirty-three years old. That could almost count as still young. To someone older at least. I didn't know anything definitely.

"I can probably do this," I said.

"Of course you can." She smiled at me. "What I am doing, this is what men do. Only I do it better."

"You do," I agreed.

She slipped off my underwear. I lay back on her futon. It was in the same place where I had kept my futon. For all I knew, it was my futon. I closed my eyes. I could not quite believe how good it felt, her fingers touching me, her lips on mine. I came much too quickly, my whole body shaking. I was embarrassed. My new friend lay on her side, watching me. I still did not know her name. I felt at that moment that if she let me, I would love her. I could live with her in this room that had once been mine, I could go back in time. I could go back to the office, go out for lunch with Judy and tell her that I had become a lesbian and she would laugh at me.

"I love to make women come," my new friend said.

I was still catching my breath.

"You are really good at it," I said.

"Maybe I can put that on my résumé," she said. "I need a better job."

I laughed. I was feeling more comfortable, already.

"I have to go," she said. "I actually only have a couple of hours until work."

"Where do you work?"

She said a place and I gave her a blank look. "I am a waitress, but really, I am a writer."

I had forgotten. This was San Francisco where every single white girl you met had majored in English and wanted to be a writer. Even the lesbians.

I felt a certain impatience emanating from her. "Shouldn't I do something for you?" I asked.

"Nope," she said. "No time. Also you couldn't."

"I could," I said, like a petulant child.

I did not like how the energy in the room had changed. I was being sent away. I did not know how I ended up in her bed, but I wanted to lay under the covers and go to sleep. My new friend seemed to understand my thoughts.

She handed me my dress.

"Oh," I said.

"I really am sorry," she said. "I have a girlfriend. She is already pissed at me. She says all I have to do is blink and I cheat on her."

"You have a girlfriend?" I asked, jealous. I had forgotten that I had a husband.

"And I promised. I told her, no more girls. But there you were," she said, helping me into my underwear as if I was a little girl. "Standing on my doorstep, dressed like a present I had to unwrap."

She looked at those boxes. "You should probably take them with you."

I looked at them. Did I want these things? "Can I come back for them later?"

She looked at her watch. "I don't think that is such a good idea," she said. "Especially if Phoebe already kicked you out."

"I don't know your name," I said.

"Lea," she said.

"My name is Leah," I said.

"That is too weird," she said.

"How do you spell it?" I asked her.

"L-E-A."

"I spell mine with an H."

"Still weird," Lea said. "I mean, it's not that common."

It wasn't. There had been six Jennifers in my sixth-grade class. I could not remember ever meeting another Leah, spelled any which way. I wondered if that meant she would let me stay. This was stupid. Lea had made her position clear. I did not want to cause trouble for her. I was already in trouble. It was not a good feeling.

"So you'll be able to carry these?" the other Lea said, standing up.

I felt sad. I did not want to talk about leaving. I wanted to talk about our names some more. Was she named after someone in her family? Her paternal grandmother, like me? Did Lea know the Hebrew definition of our name meant weary?

Or patient. The patient wife of Jacob. I had never liked that. Did Lea feel like a Lea? She did not seem weary or patient or ready to ever be someone's calm and supportive wife. Her arms were too strong, muscular. I looked at the boxes. I had on those high-heeled shoes, which were already hard enough to walk in.

"I don't think so," I said. I was pretty sure I didn't want those boxes anyway.

But Lea picked up all three boxes. I followed her out of the room and down the hall. I did not offer to help.

"What about Alice?" I asked as we went past her door. I still could not remember her last name. It was possible that I never knew it. "Do you know what happened to her? She used to live here, too."

"Alice?" Lea said. "You mean poor wounded Alice, the anorexic with a heart of gold."

"She still lives here?" I was incredulous. Ten years had passed. "I thought Phoebe wanted us both gone."

"Between you and me, there is something slightly sinister going on with the two of them," Lea said. "Not healthy. Codependent in the sickest way."

I stopped where I stood. On the wall hung a painting I vaguely remembered, unfinished when I had left. Rabbits in a meadow. It wasn't particularly good. I remembered the canvas in Phoebe's room when I interviewed for the room.

"Maybe I want to say hello to Alice," I said.

"She's not here. She has group today," Lea said.

"She had group when I lived here, too."

"They are really both crazy. It is actually really good I met you today. It confirms what I already knew. I need to move out of here. But my girlfriend doesn't want me to move in with her."

"You keep making other girls come."

I felt brazen, just saying the word "come."

Lea had started already walking down the stairs and I followed behind her, shoes in my hands. What would I say to Alice now? She was still alive. Wasn't that what I had wanted to know? I had felt guilty, for years, leaving her, not knowing what happened to her, worrying, and now I knew.

"I feel like I am only going to be young right now," Lea said. I wondered what she meant, and then I remembered, she was talking about me and what we had done. I had had that thought, too. I realized that probably, if not technically, I had cheated on Hans. I wondered if it counted because I had been with a woman. If it had not been intercourse. That was what Bill Clinton had said. At the bottom of the steps, Lea put down the boxes to open the front door.

"Okay," I said. "I will help."

I took one of the boxes. But I was the one in the dress, so I let Lea carry the other two.

I followed her two blocks down Castro Street, to the place where the Victorian houses ended and the strip of stores and restaurants began. Lea hailed me a taxi. She tried to put me inside the taxi.

"This was fun," she said.

I was not sure what to say. I felt confused, almost the same sort of fear I had felt sitting in Judy's red car. It did not make sense. Lea asked the taxi driver to open the trunk and she began to put the boxes in the trunk while I watched, not sure how to end this good-bye.

She came over to the open door. She gently cupped my chin with her hand.

"You have money for a taxi, right?"

"I do," I said.

I had had this conversation so very recently. Hans had left the apartment and gone to the ATM across the street. That had been yesterday. That had not even been twenty-four hours ago. That had been in a different world.

"I could just come with you," I said. "To the café. I am a writer, too."

There, I said it.

"Good," Judy said. "A much better writer than she is, too."

"What about the boxes?" Lea asked.

"We can take the taxi to the café."

I was surprised when Lea agreed. We actually held hands in the backseat. I wondereded what it would be like, if she were my girlfriend. I could introduce her to my mother, say, This is my girlfriend, Lea. I wondered how long we would think it was funny, the way we had the same name. Lea had the taxi drop us off at a café on Valencia Street, not far from the bar where Daniel had been a bartender. I missed Valencia Street. I paid the fare. Lea carried the boxes to a tiled table in the back of the café. I carried my shoes and my bag. I watched as Lea pulled a laptop computer out of her backpack.

"You were carrying that, too?" I said, full of admiration.

"I work out," Lea said.

That, of course, was obvious. She started typing.

I was not sure what I was supposed to do. My computer was in the trunk of Diego's car. I had to do something. In one of the boxes, I found an old notebook. It was only half full. I opened to a blank page and I started writing. I figured I might as well write something. I had told Lea I was a writer. I had finished my novel, so I might as well start something new. A story, maybe. Writing in a notebook, it was something I almost never did anymore. I wrote a sentence and the words started to come. They came too quickly, and I could not keep up, writing by hand.

"You see," Judy said.

But I did not know what she meant.

You see, you are writing?

I knew I was a writer. I knew I had written a book and I even knew that it was probably good. I just wanted to keep that quiet. Make sure. Protect myself from disappointment.

You see, you are a lesbian?

You see, you should have never gotten married?

You see, you should have never left San Francisco?

It worried me that I did not understand Judy's chiding. If the voice was coming from me, wouldn't I understand my own meaning? I bit the end of my black pen, which burst onto my hand. I used a napkin to contain the ink.

"You're pretty," the other Lea said. She had stopped writing. She was appraising me. I wondered for how long. My fingers were covered in black ink.

"You have a girlfriend," I said.

"Damn." Lea laughed.

After a while, Lea told me she had to leave for work.

She touched the inside of my wrist, which made me shiver. She took a pen and wrote down her phone number. "You can call me if you need anything."

"You are so nice," I said.

I was not going to call her. Those boxes under the table,

which she had carried to the café, I was not going to take those with me either.

"You see," Judy had said.

I did not see.

It didn't seem to matter.

I liked the way my day had turned out.

IEGO WAS OUT ON A date.

It felt familiar, the realization that Diego was not available to me. I sat at Diego's kitchen table. I ate from a bowl of salted nuts. Cashews, pecans, almonds. He had good food in his apartment. I cracked open a beer. I turned on his stereo. Finally, I called Hans.

"I haven't heard from you all day," Hans said.

I took a drink from my beer. I knew that I was supposed to call him and so I called him. Already I wished that I hadn't. He could have at least pretended not to be upset with me.

"I was worried about you."

"I have been busy all day," I said. "I went to Judy's funeral."

"Was it sad?"

"Was it sad?"

I was not sure. Already, it felt like a long time ago. I thought funerals, by definition, were sad, and therefore it was a dumb question. I realized that I wanted to take a bath. Diego had a nice bathtub, Jacuzzi jets on the sides of the tub. Diego's life was an advertisement for getting a good job. He lived in a gorgeous condo in a new building in a neighborhood called SOMA, an area I barely knew existed when I lived in San Francisco, which was actually not far from my mechanic. Diego had a stainless steel refrigerator, two bedrooms, white walls, modern appliances, modern furniture, high ceilings, a view of the bay. It was clean. Probably he had a maid.

"I mean, no, the funeral itself wasn't sad. It took place in this beautiful barn and Judy had nice friends, people from the office came and other painters she knew. They said wonderful things about her. It made me wish I hadn't lost touch with her. That part was sad. I feel bad about that. Falling out of touch with Judy."

In the act of saying these words, I felt sad again. Why was Judy talking to me, giving me unwanted advice? When I was a terrible person. Hans would agree with this, too. For going away. For not calling. For what I had done this afternoon. I stared at Diego's refrigerator. It was silly, but one day, I knew, in my lifetime, I wanted a refrigerator just like that. I realized that there was silence on the phone line. Neither of us was talking. I was supposed to offer Hans something. I was not sure.

"She left me her red car," I said.

"The one she crashed in?"

"Yes," I said. "It's pretty messed up but the mechanic says he can fix it."

"So you are going to get her car," Hans said.

"I don't think so," I said. "I never liked the car and she died in it. How could I drive a car that Judy died in? The mechanic said he would sell it for me."

"Are you going to trust the mechanic?"

"He was wearing a Grateful Dead T-shirt," I said. I realized that Judy had not trusted him either. But I did. And I trusted my instincts. I did not feel bad about what happened with Lea. I was supposed to feel bad about Lea.

"That doesn't mean you can trust him."

"I thought you trusted Deadheads."

"Don't make fun of me, Leah."

"I'm not," I said, though I guess I was. I drank another sip of beer. Soon, I would need another one. "Anyway, I don't want the car. Judy died in it, and I got a bad feeling just sitting in it, but the mechanic says he can sell it for me."

"We could use the money."

I regretted telling Hans about the car, about the possibility of selling it. This was something Judy had left me, but if the money from the car went into our joint account, it would be absorbed, get spent on rent and food and beer. It would not be mine. Judy had left the car to me. I had not told him about the money. I did not know, still, how much money. If that part was real.

"I wrote some new scenes today," Hans said. "And a review for the website. I was wondering if you could read them."

I closed my eyes, nodding. The last thing I wanted to do was go over new work by Hans. Our writing process was different. I didn't want a reader until I was far along in a project, done with a draft. Hans wanted constant eyes and ears.

"I can read it tomorrow," I said.

"I am really jazzed about these pages," Hans said. "I think I was feeling shitty about your leaving, so I tried to figure out what would make me feel better. And that was writing. Do you think you can read the scenes tonight? I'm excited about them. What else do you have to do?"

Somehow, without noticing, I had wandered into Diego's living room. I looked at the gleaming candlestick holders on Diego's mantelpiece. They were ostentatious. I could imagine an attractive salesgirl, like the one in Macy's, urging him to buy them.

"I'll read it tomorrow," I said.

"I emailed you the file hours ago."

I had not checked my email all day, which was unlike me. At home, I spent too much of my day sitting in front of a computer. "I haven't checked my email," I said. Email at least would be better than talking to Hans. "I'll do it now."

"I love you," Hans told me.

I nodded.

The silence was long. It was heavy.

"I love you, too," I said.

I hung up the phone.

I blamed Judy for this constant state of irritation I felt toward Hans. My unwillingness to talk to him, to think about him even. The repugnance I felt. I had not felt this way until her death.

"That is total bullshit," Judy said. "Maybe it has something to do with his choking you. How about that?"

Just like that, tears welled in my eyes. I was crying again. So what? Were there rules against that? I touched my neck, gently caressed the soft skin. It wasn't bruised. No imprint. Lea, she had kissed me there. Judy knew. I thought that nobody knew. I did not want anybody to know.

"I am giving you a road map," Judy said. "I am giving you a car and an adventure. You do this. You do it for me and you do it for yourself."

I nodded. Maybe I was ready to listen to Judy. I did not think so.

Back when I was in grad school, I would question all the decisions I made: Should I take this class? Eat fish for dinner? Rent this apartment? I knew without asking what Judy would think and hearing her voice had been helpful. But once I stopped returning her emails, after I had gotten married, her voice went away, too. It occurred to me that she had been helpful.

A road map.

I let the words sink in.

I wandered Diego's apartment. I found the whiskey in a liquor cabinet stocked as if for a party. I did not want to finish my beer. It was not what I wanted. I poured a drink into a nice heavy glass and got two perfect ice cubes from the ice maker. I took half of a hydrocodone I found in his medicine cabinet. This would be the definition of a perfect night for Hans and me. A drink, a pain pill, take-in sushi, an episode of *Six Feet Under.* For Hans, this perfect night would end with sex, but so many times, I would pass out in the middle of the episode.

"Are you sleeping?" Hans would ask, and I would say no, because I actually wasn't. My eyes were closed, but I could hear still Lauren Ambrose's voice, complaining about something. I did not have to actually see her, actually watch the show. It was enough to listen. I always thought I would like to be friends with Lauren Ambrose.

It was odd to be alone in Diego's apartment. I wandered back into his living room with the idea that I would look at the books on his bookshelf. He had no bookshelves. He had no books. On closer inspection, I found a travel guide to Paris. Paris. I had been to Paris once, with Hans, for a long weekend. It had been a wonderful trip. Until I met Hans, I had never been to Europe. I had not backpacked Europe during college. We went to Venice together. We kissed in a gondola.

"You see," I said to Judy.

She did not answer.

She was dead.

Judy.

I ran water for a bath.

DIEGO SEEMED MILDLY ANNOYED WITH me.

"You know one way to end a date fast?" he asked.

His hands were under my armpits and he was gently lifting me from his wonderfully fancy bathtub. When I was standing up, balanced on my own two feet, he dried me off with a white fluffy towel.

"This is a gorgeous towel," I said.

"It's called a bath sheet," Diego said.

When I was dry, I lifted my arms and slid into the men's T-shirt he handed me.

"You are a Giants fan," I observed.

"You root for the home team," Diego said.

I remembered that he had asked me a question.

"How *do* you end a date fast?" I asked him.

"Bring home a woman. She goes into the bathroom, to get ready, if you know what I mean, and she finds a naked woman passed out in your bathtub."

"I was passed out?"

"Maybe a little bit." Diego laughed. "You know you can drown that way?"

"But I feel so happy right now," I said.

I leaned forward and kissed Diego. He returned my kiss. The only way to make any progress with Diego was to be in a state of intoxication. It was so easy really; I was essentially naked, wearing only Diego's T-shirt.

"I have always wanted you," I said.

"I know that," Diego answered.

I reached into his pants for his penis and it was already hard. It was smooth in my hand, long, different than the other penises I had known.

He did not match my declaration of longing. But he seemed entertained by me, which was a good thing. I felt like this was as close as I would ever come. Without clothes, without inhibition. Without guilt, even. There in his bathroom, Diego let me stroke his penis. I pulled on it gently. I was too tired to remain standing. I got down on my knees. I licked the tip of his penis. Diego moaned. I knew from years of experience, from Hans, and Daniel, from my Republican boyfriend in high school whose name I could not remember. This was what a man wanted.

"Oh, Leah," Diego said.

This was what I had not been able to do for the other Lea. I wish I had. I wondered if it would take a long time, because I was starting to feel cold, uncomfortable, on his tiled bathroom floor. I realized too late that what I wanted, in fact, was for Diego to make love to me. I sensed that would not happen. I did not want to be gently rejected. Not now. I remembered that other time, so many years ago. How much it had hurt, though I had pretended not to care.

So, I sucked Diego. I cupped his balls with my fingers. Diego pulled my hair. He came in my mouth, without warning, and I swallowed.

IEGO WAS GONE WHEN I woke up the next morning, not in his bed, but in the guest room. The guest room, actually, was quite lovely. He had done the coffee preparation in advance, too, with a note that said: *Push me*.

Somehow, I doubted Diego had any knowledge of *Alice in Wonderland*. I pushed the button and waited. The coffee was good. I did not know if I had a hangover, if it was jet lag, or if the fuzzy state of my head was simply the fuzzy state of my head. Honestly, I often woke up unclear.

Coffee in hand, I checked my email. The mechanic had written, asking me to call him right away. I hated that: "right away," how demanding that sounded, and I decided that he could wait until later. My mother wrote, asking if I wanted to meet for lunch later in the week. I would have to respond, tell her where I was. There were four emails from Hans. Too many emails. He had emailed a scene to read, just like he had told me. A movie review to edit. I couldn't remember what I had told him the night before. I probably told him that I would read these things, but I didn't want to. I wasn't on vacation, exactly, but I was off duty. I had work today. My part-time telecommuting job. I should do that and get it out of the way. I wanted to hang a sign around my neck: Off Duty.

Off duty.

That could maybe help explain the day before, Lea on her futon on Castro Street, Diego on the tiled floor of his bathroom. I was in San Francisco. Therefore, it did not count. Off duty. I drank my coffee. I would have to go to Judy's niece's bat mitzvah next, because what else could I do? I would follow the wishes of a dead friend. I did not remember the date. I would have to reread her letter.

"Damned straight," Judy said.

"Go away," I said, and then immediately regretted it.

The vigor was too much first thing in the morning. I was getting sick of Judy commenting on my thoughts, and never when I expected her to. Voices. I could call these voices, but schizophrenics heard voices and I did not feel crazy. Maybe I was projecting: this was what Judy would say. Anyway, I had to remember that she was trying to be helpful. She had always wanted to look out for me. It was selfish to think that she had died in order to save me. Judy had died because she had wanted to die. Somehow, she knew that other car was coming. She had wanted to be done with life, but maybe, maybe she wanted to save me, too. Maybe she had thought, *Hey, this is worth a shot.* She wrote me a letter.

Was I worth a shot?

I didn't think so.

I wasn't sure.

I poured myself more coffee. I read Hans's scene. I read it right on the screen without bothering to print it out. Using track changes, I fixed sentences, sometimes flat out rewriting them, not concerned about making them sound like his voice. I wrote some new sentences. I was beginning to feel attached to his book, to feel like it was my book. Usually, he would delete my sentences anyway. "This sounds too Leah," he would say. Anyway, it was not my book. I would write it differently. I would not write that book. I emailed him back the edited file. Boom. I felt as if I had bought myself some time.

I did not read his review. That was too much. I simply hit reply, wrote: "This is great." I hoped there were no typos.

I did not write my mother after all. Even though I knew I should. I felt restless, wanted to be away from the computer.

"What now?" I said to the empty room.

The fog had lifted. Sunlight was pouring in from the window. It was a beautiful day. Like a gift. I didn't need Judy to answer me. I had lived in San Francisco for years. I knew what to do.

THE SEA LIONS WERE STILL there, still taking over Pier 39, still putting on a wonderful show for the tourists. For me. Come on, they were there for me. I gazed at them, filled with love, filled with longing.

"Oh my god, I have missed you," I told the sea lions.

In New York, I sometimes went to the Central Park Zoo, just for the sea lions. They had three sea lions in a clear glass tank, where you could watch them swim underwater. It was a wonderful spot, but it was not the same.

I leaned on the railing and I watched them. I wanted to say that the sea lions had missed me, too, but that was going too far. The sea lions climbed on one another, jockeying for position. The sea lions slept. Slick and black and shiny from the water, they rolled over each other, and then slid into the water, coming up onto another dock, only to sleep some more. They made wonderful noises, honking loudly at one another.

I grinned at them.

They would not tell me what to do, my beloved sea lions, because they did not care about me, they did not love me, and that was also fine. They were sea lions. I was trying to figure it out. Love. Maybe it was all about love. The other Lea, for instance, who lived in my room, she did not love me. I knew where she lived, but that was not the point. She had a girlfriend.

She had told me that because she wanted to keep on having a girlfriend.

Diego did not love me. Of course, he would let me give him a blowjob. I was drunk and stoned and probably so was he. What was wrong with that? He had been on a date earlier that night. He did not bring me into his bedroom. He was amused by me, he always had been. I wondered why it wasn't more. Maybe it was because he knew we weren't right for each other. We weren't. Though I would give it a try if he let me. I would.

But Hans, Hans loved me. Hans loved me and Hans wanted me to come home. Hans wanted me, body and soul, and the idea of it was enough to make me want to cry. Why had we started dating each other in graduate school? Could I remember? I remember being lonely when I started graduate school. The UPS man delivering my boxes had asked me why I left San Francisco and I had no good answer. Why was it that I had found someone to love me and I felt like I was being strangled?

I stared at the sea lions.

I was glad they had taken over this pier.

My mother loved me.

Look at what Judy had accomplished in dying. She had gotten me back to San Francisco. So many nights, lying in bed, Hans snoring, listening to him snore and to the car alarm across the street that invariably went off every night, I used to wonder if I would ever make it back.

It felt good to be back.

"You are welcome," Judy said.

Eventually, I left the pier and walked up Columbus Avenue. It was a steep hill, and I took big breaths, as if to fill my lungs with San Francisco air.

I got a cappuccino and a slice of Sicilian pizza at an Italian café across from City Lights Books. I sat at a table outside. I felt like myself, not in an expensive funeral dress, but my own clothes again, a cotton skirt and a black T-shirt, no makeup, my long hair back in a ponytail. This didn't feel like a bad thing, being me. It seemed within the realm of reason that I could actually choose to like myself. I realized that I never wanted to go home.

"I am sorry," I said, wondering if Hans could hear me, knowing that he would not forgive me. It was just a thought, not even an actual idea. I wished that I had not had it. Because I had to go home. I had a plane ticket. I would have to go back.

"No, you don't," Judy said.

What did she know?

I shook my head. I had no answer.

"Fight with me, why don't you?" she said. "I mean it. Give me what you've got."

I hated to fight. She knew that, Judy. I shook my head. The waiter returned to my table, asked if I needed anything else. I ordered the tiramisu.

CALLED THE MECHANIC FROM A pay phone in the back of the café.

"Something strange is happening with the car," he said.

"What do you mean?"

"I mean, the car fixed itself."

"What?" I said.

"Fixed. The body of the car has, essentially, regenerated itself."

"I don't know what you are saying."

"The smashed door. The metal was like putty, like I was working with clay. The car is fixed. I painted the door. The tail light fixed itself. Car looks as good as new."

"That is impossible."

"I agree," the mechanic said. "But it is also true. So I'll try to sell it?"

I was not sure. Maybe I wanted to see it again after all.

"I might want to see it," I said.

"It's a car miracle," he said.

I decided. "I'll come see it."

"Where are you?" he asked.

"North Beach," I said.

"I tell you what," he said. "I want to drive this thing. See how it feels. I'll pick you up."

I gave him the address of my café.

"See you soon."

It seemed like an okay idea. I liked waking up and not knowing what would happen. First, the sea lions. Tiramisu. Now a car that had regenerated

"I loved that car," Judy said.

"But you died in it, Judy. You died in that car."

"Since when are you superstitious?"

She had me. But she was also wrong. There was something called karma. A car that she had died in, that had to be bad karma.

"Have an open mind," Judy said.

At least we were not fighting.

W E DROVE FROM ONE END of the city to the other. I had my seat belt on. I sat in the passenger seat. I had a driver's license but it had been years since I had driven. We drove through Golden Gate Park. We drove past the buffalo. We drove all the way to the ocean and parked. I hoped that the mechanic understood that none of this was romantic.

We walked to the edge of a cliff and looked out at the scenery. I stepped up to the edge. Hans was scared of heights. If I was with him, he would have asked me to take a step back. We had had fights before, loud yelling screaming fights, in otherwise idyllic places, when I would get too close to the edge. It was not like I was ever going to fall off a cliff.

I looked at the ocean.

Sea lions. Ocean views. It was so beautiful here, but I had left San Francisco and it was no longer my home. I really needed to call my mother. I didn't want her to worry about me.

"It feels good," the mechanic said, startling me. "Your car. A little heavy on the gas."

I had forgotten about the car. My brain was holding on to small bits of information. I had forgotten about the mechanic.

"Can you change that?" I asked him.

"Nope," the mechanic said. "This car is built to go fast."

"But you think it's safe now?" I asked.

"What do you mean?"

I did not know what I meant. "Like." I searched for the words. "The car won't spontaneously combust on the middle of a highway?" I asked. "Or start losing parts. A tire falling off while I'm on the highway. Or the door. The steering wheel coming loose in my hands. Like a bad dream. Only real."

The mechanic looked at me, confused.

"It's a good car," he said.

I looked at the ocean. It seemed impossible that Judy could be killed and that the machine that had killed her could come out unscathed. It had failed in its job to protect her. It was not a car. It was an instrument of death. That was what it was, exactly.

"But that is what I wanted," Judy told me. "You can't blame the car."

The mechanic leaned over and tried to kiss me.

I took a step away. I realized I was in a high place. I could actually fall. I sadly shook my head. It seemed unfair. After Lea. After Diego. But I did not want to kiss the mechanic.

"A guy has to try," he said.

"No, you don't," I said quietly.

I looked at the view. I took a deep breath. I realized that I had not done my job yet that day. I had not picked the news.

"Go do your job," Judy said.

I was glad that the voice of Judy was still prudent. Focusing on the small things. She did not want me to fall off a cliff.

"I am on your side," Judy said.

Earlier that day, she had wanted to fight.

"I have to go," I told the mechanic. I felt sympathetic toward the mechanic. He had been kind to me.

"It's a nice view," he said.

"I still have to go."

"You still want to sell the car?" he asked.

"I don't know."

"Insurance will pay for the repairs. I submitted the claim," he said.

"That's good," I said. "Thanks."

"Okay then."

I nodded. Something had changed. The mechanic. Maybe he seemed angry. I wanted to leave.

"You want to drive?" he asked me.

"It's been a long time," I said.

We walked back to the car. It was my red car, restored, a present from the dead. I got behind the wheel. I hoped for a moment of epiphany: a sense of empowerment, driving my red car though San Francisco. The car, though, it was heavy on the gas. This time, I noticed the smell. Judy's flowery perfume. It smelled like Judy. Though earlier I had been fine as a passenger, in the driver's seat, I felt as if I could not breathe. The feeling came over me suddenly. I realized I was driving too fast. I was afraid.

"Pull over," the mechanic said.

He could see right away that I was in trouble, gripped with terror, my foot pressed on the gas. I could kill us both but that wasn't what I wanted to do.

"Right now," the mechanic said, his voice firm. "Signal and pull over. It's safe. You don't even have to look. No one is there. Trust me."

I did what he said. I rushed out of the car and took deep

breaths. The last thing I wanted to do was throw up, there on the sidewalk.

"I am okay," I said. I felt embarrassed. Inexplicably miserable. I walked around to the passenger side and got back into Judy's red car.

"I am going to take this baby back to the shop," the mechanic said. "I'll drive you back to where you are staying."

I nodded. "Judy died in this car," I said. "The car wanted to kill her. It is not a good car. It is a murderer."

"Sweetheart, that sounds a little bit outlandish to me," the mechanic said.

"This car had it out for her from the start."

"It's just a car."

"I don't know." Saying them out loud, the words sounded outlandish to me, too. "I don't think so."

I waited for Judy to say something, but she held back. The mechanic drove the car back to the shop. The joy of driving, it was gone. I did not look out the window. Whatever we passed, the Victorian houses, the hippies on Haight Street, the street-cars on Market Street, I did not see it.

"I would drive the car to where you are staying and give you the keys, but I don't think you can drive it."

I wanted to disagree with him. I wanted to be all done with this mechanic, but he was right. Anyway, his shop was close to Diego's apartment.

"Do you want to have dinner with me tonight?" he asked, when he pulled up to the curb.

"No," I said, shaking my head. "Sorry."

I didn't feel right. I still felt whatever I felt. I had my window open wide, letting out the bad air, but it didn't make a difference. Like there was a toxic gas filling the interior and I couldn't breathe. The mechanic was unaffected. My leg shook nervously.

"It's okay," he said. "You don't have to go out with me. You don't have to sweat it."

I managed to laugh. I sort of liked it, that the mechanic still wanted to go out with me. That he wasn't angry. It was just that I couldn't breathe properly.

"Thanks," I said.

I got out of the car, unsteady on my feet. The earth was unsteady; the piece of land in which I stood was on a steep angle. San Francisco and its hills. I actually lost my footing and fell, landing on my ass. It was embarrassing. I hated falling. I got back up. I shrugged as if I was not embarrassed. I looked at the ground.

"You take it easy," the mechanic said.

He drove off in Judy's car. My car. I owned that red car. Maybe Judy hadn't wanted to die. Maybe the car had wanted to kill her.

"Ridiculous," Judy said.

I had read her letter only once but the words stayed with me. She had wanted to die. The car listened to her thoughts, complied with her wishes. Maybe I had been reading too many Haruki Murakami novels. I let myself into Diego's apartment and sank down to the floor. I wished that Diego had a cat. I would have given anything at that moment to pet a cat.

DID MY TELECOMMUTING JOB.

It was ingrained in me, the desire not to get in trouble. I was three hours late, and so with the time difference, six hours late, but I would probably get away with it. I picked news stories, fixed headlines. There were things happening in the world. Everything I knew, I knew from my job. I knew about the pharmaceuticals market. I knew if stocks were up or down. I knew if it was football season or baseball. I knew the top film at the box office each week and what was happening in the Middle East. It was a good job. Today, opening the feed for finance, I picked a story about Jonathan Beene, founder of the hot tech crowdsourcing company currently changing the state of micro-financing. He was giving a speech at Stanford.

Funny, I thought.

It was weird to me, how rich he was. How successful. I wouldn't have guessed it. If he had not become famous, it is possible I would not have thought of him at all. Sometimes I wondered if I ever published a novel, who would remember me. Would Jonathan Beene think to himself, *I once slept with her. Had a crush on her. Paid to have sex with her, though really she wasn't worth it.* It was a stupid place to let my imagination go, but that was where it went.

I wrote a short email to my current boss, Scottie, who was

not dead, and I told him that I had gone to San Francisco at the last minute for a funeral and apologized for doing my work late and expressed my apologies if any clients had complained. Hopefully that had not happened, but I was covering my bases. I also asked if it was possible if I could take some time off, if someone could cover my shifts while I was away.

"Good girl," Judy said.

She was back.

I was glad.

I was so glad.

I sat at Diego's kitchen table, as if glued to the seat of the chair, waiting for something. I did not know what. I had already been to see the sea lions. I was out of ideas. Was it a coincidence that I had picked a news story about Jonathan Beene? Or was it a sign, something I should follow? I felt as if Judy was telling me to follow signs. Most of my life, I had willfully ignored them. I wondered if I should take a shower. I wanted to, but the bathroom in Diego's apartment was all the way down the hall. It was a long hallway. I was having trouble getting out of the chair. A day, a day could be long, longer than anything. Diego would not be home from work for hours and hours. I knew that I should call Hans. I did not want to call Hans.

I wrote to my mother. It was easy enough to do. I did not have to get up. I should have done it sooner. I told her where I was and what had happened to Judy and when I would be coming home. I sent her Diego's phone number in case she wanted to reach me. I also left out parts. The fight I had had with Hans. The other Lea. Judy's red car. I told her that I loved her. I hit send.

"Good girl," Judy said.

"I know," I said. "I know that I am."

"You suffer from a lot of doubt."

That was also true.

I did a lot of not so good things, but somehow I did not doubt my goodness. Still, I didn't mind Judy's praise. Maybe it could be said that I had done several not so good things in just the last couple of days. I wondered if I were to track down the other Lea, if she would be happy to see me. If not on her futon, at her favorite café. I could bring my computer. I could simply go to her favorite café. It was a good one. I could go there and work my novel. Lea would not mind.

But my computer looked at me, as if to say, *Fuck you.*

"It's true," I said to my computer.

I was talking to my computer now.

"Follow the signs," Judy said.

WALKED BACK TO THE MECHANIC'S shop.

He was sitting at his desk. His office smelled like marijuana. Clichés, they so often proved to be true. Though most Deadheads were not mechanics. I would have avoided him if I could but he held the keys to my car.

"Why do you do this job?" I asked him.

"I am good at it," he said.

That answer did not quite satisfy me.

"What?" he said. "I am supposed to follow the Dead? I did that, you know, and then Jerry died. I am done with that scene. I want nice things in my life. I decided a long time ago that I was done crashing on other people's couches. I am good with my hands," he said. "I play guitar, too, but that doesn't pay for shit."

It was unnerving to see my Deadhead mechanic in a sardonic mood. I did not think the pot was treating him well. "Why are you here?" he asked.

"I want the keys," I said.

He took them out of his back pocket and handed them to me. I wanted this mechanic not to be angry at me. I reminded myself that he did not actually matter.

"How much do I owe you?" I asked him.

"The car fixed itself," he said.

"I forgot about that."

"I didn't."

"I don't owe you any money?"

"Are you going to argue with me?"

I was not.

"I also put in a sizable quote to the insurance company," he said.

I nodded. That made more sense.

"Thank you," I said. "For everything."

This sounded overly formal to me, but I was saying good-bye. I didn't want the mechanic in my life anymore. He was fine. He was familiar. He somehow bugged the shit out of me. I did not owe him anything.

"Drive safe," he said.

I went into the garage and found Judy's red car. It looked fine. The car was ten years old and had been nearly totaled in an accident but looked shiny and new. I put the keys into the ignition. I put the car in drive. I cautiously pulled out into the street.

"It won't hurt you," Judy said.

"Okay," I said. I wasn't sure.

"Are you going to Stanford?" she asked.

"Tomorrow," I said. "The speech is tomorrow. I am going."

"Good," she said. "I am glad you are going."

"Why did you kill yourself?" I asked her.

It was a dumb thing to ask, especially on a road that suddenly took a steep nosedive. I hit the brakes too hard and the car behind me screeched to a stop, honking his horn. I could hear a man's voice shouting at me, "Learn to drive, motherfucker."

It was only half a mile back to Diego's apartment, straight

downhill. I barely let myself touch the gas pedal. I did not die. I parked the car in Diego's parking space. Judy did not answer my question. She did not speak when spoken to. I walked to the Mission District, looking for a place to eat. I did not go to my favorite burrito place because the line was too long. I did not go to La Cumbre with the painting of the whore on the tables because I did not want to see another ghost, run into the boyfriend who was not a boyfriend. I went to another taqueria, a place that had been my third favorite, because the line was not long. The burrito was not as good as I remembered the burritos of my youth to be. It was actually bad. Somehow, I thought this was my fault. I had picked unwisely.

"It's just a burrito," Judy said.

THE NEXT MORNING, I DROVE Judy's car to Palo Alto.

Why shouldn't I go to Stanford, sit in the back row, listen to Jonathan Beene's lecture? I was following the signs.

When necessary, it turned out that I could be competent. I could drive the red car, even on a highway. While it was admittedly difficult for me to switch lanes, once positioned in the correct lane, I found that I did not have to switch out of it. Even when the lane suddenly slowed. Or when I got stuck behind a large oil tank. I pictured disaster, a leak and then a sudden bursting into flames. I took my time. Judy's red car wanted to go fast, but I drove slowly.

"Good car," I repeated under my breath, as if I was talking to a dog. "Good car. Good car."

I kept the windows open. I ignored the smell.

An hour later, I pulled into the driveway of my friend Margaret's house. As far as I knew, she had not moved. Margaret had been a graduate student at Stanford in anthropology and was given a postdoc after she received her PhD to continue her research. She had lived on my hall freshman year at Haverford. When I was shunned after the Jonathan Beene scandal, she emerged and offered support. I thought she was boring at the time. She was from the Midwest. She had a steady boyfriend from her hometown. She had hair the color of toast and wore clothes that she bought at discount stores. She studied all the time. Like everyone else at Haverford College, she was earnest and sincere. Ethical. Still, she liked me. She sent me letters when I transferred to Rutgers. She remembered my birthday. We didn't see each other much when I lived in San Francisco. She had gone to Zanzibar to do her fieldwork. She taught undergraduate classes. She wrote academic papers and then her dissertation. She worked hard.

Margaret was not expecting me and yet she did not seem all that surprised to see me either. She rubbed her eyes, staring at the red car parked in her driveway.

"Gosh," she said. "Is that yours?"

I shrugged. "I am not sure," I said.

"I thought you were scared of driving."

Margaret had a good memory. Of course, we were friends. I realized it right away and this made me happy. I had known her for a long time. It turned out that my legs were shaking. My breathing was shallow. My body had worked with me, waiting to have its panic attack until the moment I got out of Judy's car.

"Oh my god, what am I doing?" Margaret was wearing striped leggings and a kitten T-shirt. She opened the door and hugged me. "Leah! Leah, Leah, Leah."

Margaret was glad to see me. She always seemed like such an odd friend that at some point, surely, she would figure out that we had nothing in common, that she did not even like me.

"You're shaking," she said.

"I haven't driven in a long time," I said.

I sat down on the front step of Margaret's house and breathed. The shaking slowly stopped. Margaret sat next to me. The sky in Palo Alto was a brilliant blue, luminescent clouds in the sky.

A woman in a minivan pulled out from the house next door. She slowed down to look at me. There was a little girl in a car seat in the back.

"Everything okay?" she asked Margaret.

Margaret nodded. "My friend Leah just drove in from San Francisco. It's the first time she's driven in years."

I nodded.

"And the car is haunted," I said. "Possessed, maybe. I am not sure."

Margaret tilted her head to the side. The woman in the minivan did not hear me. She waved at Margaret and left.

"You are wearing a really nice dress," Margaret said.

I was. I was wearing my funeral dress. I had looked at all the clothes in my carry-on bag that morning and I had not wanted to wear any of them. I did not know why. I thought I would wear the dress to Jonathan's lecture, even though it was still hours away.

"You are getting it dirty," Margaret said.

I shrugged. The steps seemed clean.

"I have been up all night," Margaret said. "Someone from the department had these mushrooms that he picked doing fieldwork in South America and I guess I have been tripping all night. I didn't believe anything would actually happen. Isn't that crazy?"

It did not sound like Margaret.

"It was totally weird," Margaret said. "And fun. I actually had a brilliant idea and I have been writing like crazy. My fingers hurt. Look at them." She held out her fingers for me to see. "Are they red?"

"They look fine," I said.

"They do," Margaret said, holding her hands out and looking at her fingers. "They have been my best friends, these fingers, no sleep, just dancing over the keyboard. I wish I could give them something. A present."

"Maybe a hand massage," I said.

"Maybe," Margaret said.

The woman in the minivan had been right to stop. We were both a little bit off, but it was nice to see Margaret like this, so un-Margaret-like.

"I have something to tell you," Margaret said. She actually giggled.

"What?"

"I am in love."

"With who?"

"Do you remember Yannick?"

I did. He was the unattainable graduate student in her department. The one who Margaret wanted, half French, half black, gorgeous, who was having an affair with a married woman. He was the program darling, a genius, the star of the department.

At that moment, Yannick emerged from Margaret's house. He was also wearing a pink kitten T-shirt. Boxer shorts. He wore his hair in dreadlocks.

"Leah." He called my name.

We had met before. I had spent a weekend in this house years ago, when I was in between apartments. I could not believe he was with Margaret or that they were wearing matching kitten T-shirts. The surprise of it all made me smile. Made me think that I never did know what could happen.

"I love those T-shirts," I said. "Would you have some more?"

Margaret started cracking up.

"We do," she said. Yannick also started laughing. I did not get the joke.

"It's so nice to see you," Yannick said. "You look so pretty. I like that dress."

It was nice that he remembered me. I was suddenly glad that Jonathan Beene's lecture had led me here, to these old friends. I looked at Margaret, worried she would be upset Yannick had praised my appearance. She seemed fine.

"Did you write me? Tell me you were coming?" Margaret asked.

I shook my head.

"But you're going to Jonathan Beene's thing?" she asked.

Margaret had taken one of my hands. Yannick the other. We walked into Margaret's house. There was a Ping-Pong table covered with books in the dining room.

"Tessa moved out," Margaret said. "Most of the furniture was hers."

"Do you live here?" I asked Yannick.

It occurred to me that Margaret had not written me in a long time. I had not written her. I had gone quiet after I had gotten married. I was not sure why. My life had gotten less newsworthy. It felt as if everything hinged on that one file on my computer. If it was a novel, if it was a good novel, if that would work out for me.

It was a nice house that Margaret lived in. Big rooms, plush carpeting, an enormous kitchen, even if it was not furnished in the way you would expect an almost professor to live. By now, she must have been hired. There, on the Ping-

Pong table, next to a tall stack of books, was a box full of kitten T-shirts.

"What size do you want?" Yannick asked.

"Extra large," I said and then I reconsidered. "Large."

Yannick handed me one and I slipped it on over my dress. The house was strangely air-conditioned and I realized I was cold.

"I am going to make coffee," Margaret said.

It was the first thing she had said that had sounded normal since I had gotten there.

"Great," I said.

I wanted to act cool, somehow, to not be surprised that Yannick and Margaret were living together. I did not understand the T-shirts. I was proud of myself for driving Judy's car to Margaret's house. I was so proud of myself but it seemed silly to talk about it. Margaret knew about Jonathan Beene's lecture. Margaret also knew about me and Jonathan Beene. My leg had started shaking. My thoughts were racing.

"It's okay," Judy said. "Let them race."

Margaret went to make the coffee. She had one of those little metal espresso-maker things you put on a stove. It was not what I wanted. But it was also coffee.

"I am so happy to see you," Margaret said, rubbing her eyes.

She had taken mushrooms, I remembered. I had done a lot of things in my life, but I had never done that.

"I have Valium," Yannick said to me. "If you need one."

"Okay," I said. Obviously, it was apparent that I might need one. "Yes. Please."

This seemed like a good idea to me after the drive in Judy's red car, though I felt slightly ashamed to be accepting one in front of Margaret. Yannick picked up a pill bottle from the Ping-Pong table.

"What do you think?" Yannick said. "The new improved me. Committed to an available woman, a woman who loves me. A smart woman. I am on medication. I am a veritable drugstore."

"I approve," I said.

Though I wasn't entirely sure. It didn't come out sounding right, Yannick's words, the implication that he needed to be on medication to be with Margaret. I hope that was not what he meant. I was grateful for the pill.

"Yannick," Margaret said. "Leah just got here. Too much information. Too much sharing."

"There is a level of shame," Yannick said, "regarding pharmaceuticals. It is not my area of interest but, as I am currently taking psychotropics, I am interested."

"Did you take mushrooms last night, too?" I asked.

"I did," Yannick said. "Would you like one? We might have some left. I could look."

These were the smartest people in the department at one of the best universities in the country. Margaret had studied so hard as an undergraduate, never partied, never stayed out late, went to Quaker meeting.

"I'm good," I said.

Margaret handed me a small cup of coffee. I thought about it for a second, wondering about the pill in my hand, and then I swallowed it with my coffee.

"Why do you have so many kitten T-shirts?" I asked.

"I bought a box of them last weekend at a garage sale," Yannick said, as if that were the most obvious thing.

"I am so happy you are here," Margaret said, again, squeezing my free hand, almost making me spill my coffee.

"You said that already," Yannick said.

It was almost a relief to me to recognize the Yannick I had met years before; he had struck me as a pompous asshole. Now I was glad to see traces of the old him. He was the old Yannick and the new Yannick. Like Margaret. I didn't use to believe that people could change.

"But I am." Margaret grinned at me. "So glad. It has been much too long. I've missed you."

"I missed you, too," I said.

I wondered. Had I missed Margaret? I had known her for a long time but I never quite believed she really liked me. I thought her friendship was more like loyalty. What would a Haverfordian do? What did I know? I hadn't missed Hans and we were married. I had been gone for three days. But already I was missing Diego, wondering why I had left his apartment without saying good-bye. Did I write a note? He was gone when I woke up. He worked fourteen-hour days. I had always known, in theory, that people did that. That was how they got stainless steel refrigerators.

"I am going to sleep," Margaret said. "For like ten hours. And then we will catch up on everything. You can tell me about marriage and life in New York. We can go out for dinner and then we can go to Jonathan's thing. Is that okay?"

"You're going to sleep?"

It was not entirely okay with me, but this was a declaration on Margaret's part. Her eyes were bloodshot, already closing. I was not sure what I was expected to do, how I would get through the day. I could drive back to San Francisco still and skip Jonathan Beene's lecture. I did not have to follow the signs.

"Stella moved out, too," Margaret said. "If you want, you can crash in her room. She left her bed. One day I plan to buy real grown-up furniture but I am so busy."

Stella had been her other roommate. She was an English PhD candidate. Her favorite color was lilac and her hair was very straight. Why did I remember that?

"It's the morning," I said. "I don't need to sleep."

Margaret started to rub her eyes again. "I am sorry," she said. "I wouldn't have stayed up all night if I knew you were coming, but I have to sleep now."

"Me, too," Yannick said. "I am so sleepy."

He took Margaret's hand, rubbed it. He looked at her like he loved her. It looked nice. It looked like Margaret wanted him to come with her. It was almost hard to imagine, having that.

"You can eat anything you want. Read anything you want. There are bikes in the garage. I don't know if there are helmets."

"I am not going to ride a bike," I said.

"You already drove that car," Margaret said. "That so doesn't look like you. That red car."

"I know," I said. "Do you think I could use your phone? The Internet?"

"Anything," Margaret said. "Take a shower. Use my shampoo. I have Aveda shampoo."

Margaret remembered how I loved Aveda shampoo. And I would. I would use her shampoo. Yannick gently banged into

Margaret, pushing her away from me into the bedroom. I was a step behind them, following them to their door, unsure about being left alone.

"Sleep," he said to Margaret. "Let's sleep like the gods."

The door shut gently in my face.

It's what I had wanted, wasn't it? To be alone.

CHECKED MY EMAIL.

Another four new emails from Hans. An email from my mother. One from Scottie. Diego. An email from a literary agent whose name I recognized. I stared at the computer. It seemed obvious which email to read first, but I didn't.

Diego wanted to know where I was. He had been calling to check on me. He was worried. "We will go out for dinner," he wrote.

My mother was no longer worried about me now that she knew where I was. She sent her love. Her sympathy. She had met Judy, only once. We had all gone out for drinks when my mother came to visit. They had commiserated about me, what a frustrating person I could be. Mortifying, that was how I remembered it. "Be good to yourself," my mother wrote. "I envy you. San Francisco."

I had taken my mother to the sea lions when she visited. I had taken her to the bar where Daniel had worked and he had given her a shot of tequila. She drank it. I had had a life here, before graduate school, and then it had become my past, and suddenly I had all of these memories.

I opened one email from Hans. "Call me," it read. "I love you." I closed it. I did not read the others. I knew that he loved me. That wasn't it. It wasn't what I wanted to hear. I did not know what he could say. He had already apologized. I had already forgiven him. There were, I noticed, more documents attached.

I read Scottie's email. It was understanding. He gave me time off and offered his condolences.

"Are you going to read it?" Judy asked me. "What are you waiting for?"

The email from the agent. That was what she meant. I knew. "When I am ready," I said.

"I was ready ten minutes ago."

"Give me a break," I said. "Really."

I read my email from the agent. I had not queried this agent. He had read a short story I had published in a literary journal. My only published short story. He wanted to know if I was working on something. He wanted to know if I had representation.

"Look at that," Judy said.

I smiled, but then I frowned.

"It doesn't mean a thing," I said.

"It means they are coming to you."

"Is that what it means?"

Judy didn't answer. That was what she did when she was annoyed with me. My dead boss, my dead friend, constantly annoyed with me. She was wrong. It was not what it meant. Still, it was promising. This agent was young. He had sold some books. I looked him up on Google. He was wearing a suit. He looked like an agent. He was cute. Up until now, this trip, it hadn't been an issue, the attractive quotient of other people. I was married. I did not really exist. At least that was how I felt.

It was quiet in the bedroom. I didn't know why I was worried. It was too quiet. They had taken the mushrooms, the Valium, and I wanted to make sure they were okay. It was like I was a babysitter again, checking to make sure I hadn't somehow killed the baby. I gently opened the door. Margaret and Yannick were spooned together, on top of the covers, in their matching kitten T-shirts.

It seemed obvious, suddenly, what I was supposed to do. I was supposed to open the file that contained my novel and start reading it. I was following the signs. There was a literary agent out there who wanted to read something I had written. I had written something. It made no sense to me, how insanely nervous I was about doing such an obvious thing. But I had taken Yannick's pill. I did not have to be nervous because, really, I felt calm. I felt like I could float above my file and read it, like a ghost.

"You know I am not a ghost," Judy said.

"Whatever," I said. "You are not a ghost. I don't know what you are."

"Read," she said.

I got stuck on my first sentence. Did it need a comma? It currently did not have one. I added it. I looked at the sentence. It was better. I kept reading. It had been long enough that I did not remember some of the sentences. I had written this, I thought to myself in wonder. I was pleased. I added a new sentence and three paragraphs later, I found the same sentence. I deleted the first one, kept the new one. They were the same.

I wondered if there was something good to eat in Margaret's house. I found half a tray of brownies in the kitchen. Margaret has always liked making brownies. I cut off a small piece, ate it standing at the counter, cut off a much larger piece and settled back down with my computer on the couch. I wrote another sentence only to realize that it was there again, two lines down.

"Stop editing," Judy said. "Read."

But she was wrong. I fixed sentences as I went because that was how I worked. Even if I was creating extra work for myself. At least I was working. It was how I had written this book, in small stretches of time. It had taken more than two years. Almost three. I knew I hadn't imagined it, but it was somehow realer than I had thought. And I thought it was good. I did. I couldn't see myself, sitting alone in the spacious living room of Margaret's big rented house, but I knew that I was smiling. I stroked the kitten on my pink T-shirt.

"Meow," Judy said.

ARGARET, YANNICK AND I WENT to the lecture together.

"This is the first time I have ever stepped foot in the Business School," Yannick said. "Now I understand all the people I see on campus. This is where they go."

Yannick was being openly started at, with his dreadlocks and his pink kitten T-shirt. Margaret had put on a black sweater and black jeans. Her hair tucked back behind her ears, she looked like a young professor. I was wearing my funeral dress. I was glad to have these friends with me.

"How did you know about it?" I asked Margaret.

"Jonathan Beene is probably the most famous Haverford alumnus right now," Margaret said. "And I am on an email list of 'Fords in California."

"Have you been in touch with him?"

Margaret shook her head. "We aren't friends," she said. "But we do have friends in common. He knows that I am at Stanford."

"He does?"

Suddenly, I wasn't sure why I was there. Because Judy had told me to follow the signs. Because she had died. Because Hans had choked me. It had only happened that one time and it was an aberration, but somehow, it also was not a complete surprise either, when I thought about it, though I did not want to think about it, and I had not forgotten, not yet, and it seemed like he was writing me too many emails, not allowing me to forget. But that did not explain why I was at Stanford for a lecture given by Jonathan Beene. Jonathan Beene was an asshole.

The auditorium was full. I didn't really like the look of the people in the audience, ridiculously young and eager. I wished I were wearing something else, not a black dress. Maybe my kitten T-shirt.

"Is there intrigue I don't know about?" Yannick asked.

I looked at Margaret. I wasn't a good liar. She wasn't either.

"They went out. Freshman year."

"I would not call what happened between us going out," I said. Which was more than I had ever said to Margaret, because what happened between me and Jonathan Beene was not something I ever talked about.

"You tend to keep things bottled inside," Judy said.

"He was in love with you," Margaret said.

There, Margaret had said it. As if she knew something that I did not. She had never met Hans.

"He wasn't," I said.

Yannick nodded, like it all made sense to him.

"Why is he so famous, again?" I asked Margaret. I had not forgotten, but I wanted to hear what Margaret would say. "Do you know?"

"Innovations in technology," Margaret said. "He went from a simple idea, from a small invention to being a Fortune 500 company. And he's famous for his philanthropy."

"Of course he is," I said.

"Most of the projects are for individuals to finish personal

projects," Margaret said. "Independent movies, art installa-
tions. Record albums. But there is also the microfinancing.
Two percent of every contribution to someone's art project
funds a woman in a third world country, a small business. It's
twofold. A filmmaker makes a movie that shows at Sundance.
A woman buys a washing machine, starts her own laundry."

That seemed so Haverford to me. If Jonathan Beene was
the kind of success that he seemed to be, I wanted him to be
evil. For him to morally bankrupt, despicable. But when he
came up on the stage, he was just Jonathan Beene. He was still
a little bit short. He was wearing a blue blazer, jeans, no tie,
kind of dressed like he was still in college, still a nerd. Cute.
As if he had grown into his nerdiness. He seemed awkward on
the stage. I smoothed the front of my dress.

Jonathan made a speech about innovation, about dreaming
and also staying true to your dreams. "Following your heart,"
he said, "can also mean earning a lot of money. They are not
diametrically opposed as much as people seem to believe."

The connection was a surprise. At least, it seemed like a bit
of a leap to me. So far, it was also not true, at least in my case.
Jonathan's eyes wandered as he talked, to the ceiling, to the
back of his fingers, to the exit sign above the side door. It was
almost as if he wanted to flee. His speech was well written, but
he was not a good speaker.

"Why is he here?" I whispered to Margaret.

"On Earth?" Yannick asked.

"No." I felt like it would be not long before I was officially
annoyed with Yannick. "At Stanford?"

"The Business School invited him," Margaret said.

"Did he go here?" I asked.

"He dropped out of the MBA program," Margaret said.

"What did he major in?" I whispered. "In college."

I thought it was philosophy, but here he was, a prominent leader in business. How did that reconcile? Jonathan had actually written me a couple of times while I was at Rutgers but I never answered. Margaret was really the only person I still knew from that period in my life, and it had just been by chance really that we started a new friendship, running into each other in Golden Gate Park.

"Philosophy," Margaret said.

I had never picked up a philosophy text again, not after Haverford.

There was a slide show going on behind Jonathan's head. Figures. Pie graphs. The photo of an African woman wearing a head scarf, grinning as she cut the red tape on a new business. I heard the words "sustainability" followed by "profit margins." Jonathan Beene's wandering eyes landed on Yannick's dreadlocks and then Margaret—he smiled at Margaret—and then, finally, on me. Jonathan Beene stopped talking, midsentence. He knocked over his glass of water on the podium. He asked for a paper towel or something to clean up the water, and then somehow he dropped the water glass, which shattered on the wood stage, sharp slivers of glass landing on the stage and the floor.

"Excellent," Yannick said.

Margaret squeezed my hand.

Jonathan Beene was openly staring at me, his face a question mark. Was I still angry with him? That seemed silly. It was so long ago. He did not exist for me. He was not even a part of my thoughts.

Judy snorted.

A young woman quickly appeared onstage and began to clean up the glass; she clearly wasn't janitorial staff, probably a graduate student. She was wearing a blue suit and a blue headband, but was on her hands and knees with a dustpan. I wished they had sent a guy to clean up the mess. Jonathan Beene stepped away from the podium, waiting for her to be done. He continued to stare.

It was completely uncool on his part. He was a multimillionaire. I thought by now he must be cool. But he must have been surprised to see me. I was surprised to be there, too. I tried to remember what day of the week it was. It escaped me. I worried that I had forgotten to pick the news and then remembered I had taken time off. We stared at each other. I absently pulled a strand of hair into my mouth.

"Bad habit," Judy said.

I pulled the hair away. I did not like to be criticized. That was the kind of thing Hans would point out. My mother.

"Sorry," Judy said.

I appreciated the apology.

"Well," Jonathan Beene said to the audience, the stage clean. The images still brightened the screen behind his head. "I think I have said all that I want to say. Thank you for having me."

He was still looking at me. I thought he might cry.

Poor Jonathan Beene, I thought. Which was funny, considering.

ARGARET, YANNICK AND I ARGUED about going to the reception. "There is a reception?" I said.

No one had told me there was a reception. My plan had been simply to go to the lecture. To sit in the back of the room, observe. Nothing more. It had not occurred to me that Jonathan Beene would see me.

"The signs," Judy said.

"He clearly wants to talk to you," Margaret said.

"He is so in love with you," Yannick said.

"You are so not a genius," I said to Yannick.

"Whoever said that?" Yannick gave Margaret a dirty look. I felt bad. I didn't want to make trouble between them. I just did not appreciate his running commentary.

"You say that about yourself all the time Yannick," Margaret said.

"Well, that's different," Yannick said. "That is me mocking my intellect."

I just wanted off of the Stanford campus. I wanted out of the situation I had gotten myself into.

"I want to go home," I said, but I realized I didn't know where that was. Not Margaret's rented house. Not Diego's condo. Not the apartment in Queens that I shared with Hans.

I didn't want to go there either. I did not have a home. I wanted off of the campus.

"I want to leave," I said.

Margaret looked at her watch. "Let's go for a drive. Or we can take you home, Leah, and still make it back for the reception."

"We are not invited to business parties," Yannick said.

"I was." I looked at Margaret. "I told you," she said. "He knows I am at Stanford. He invited me. Haverford is a small community."

"I was kicked out," I told Yannick.

"You left," Margaret said gently.

We drove back to Margaret's house. She pulled past Judy's red car in front of the house and into the driveway.

"That car is yours?" Yannick asked. "Let's go for a motherfucking drive."

"You don't talk like that," Margaret said.

Yannick also did not have a driver's license.

"I don't want to drive it," I said.

"Well, I do," Margaret said.

"THIS CAR WANTS TO GO fast," Margaret said.

"Don't," I said.

I found myself crossing my fingers.

"I used to drive fast, back in Illinois," she said. "Back in the cornfields."

This was something I did not know about her. Yannick seemed surprised, too. I was sitting in the backseat. It was the first time I had ever sat there. It was beyond uncomfortable. My knees were pretty much even with my head. Yannick checked his seat belt.

"Maybe you should drive a little bit slower, Margaret," he said.

"Judy liked to drive fast," I said. "But not like this."

They didn't hear me. Maybe I was whispering. We also had the windows open, the radio on. I needed to tell her, to tell her what had happened to me, driving. How the mechanic helped me pull over. But I didn't say anything. I did not know why. Maybe I was curious, wanted to see what would happen, what Judy's car would do. Margaret was displaying, once again, a new side to her, one I did not like. A Bruce Springsteen song came on, but Bruce Springsteen was always on the radio, there was nothing unusual about that.

"I love this song," Margaret said, pressing on the gas. We

were on Highway 101, going much too fast. I could not see the speedometer from the backseat. At least, I thought, I would not have to explain myself to Hans if I died in a car accident. This way, he could mourn me and it would be easy, easier than getting a divorce, packing up my apartment. I would never look at my novel again. I looked out the window. It was an ugly highway, industrial. If this were the movies, speeding toward our death, we would at least be on Highway 1, driving by the ocean. Judy's red car would be a convertible. Judy had died in this car. I still didn't know why she wanted me to have it. I did not want to die in her car. Please, I thought.

"Slow down," I said to Margaret, loudly this time, but she could not hear me because of a police siren.

"Something strange is happening," Margaret said.

She was nervous now, I could see it in her fingers, the way she gripped the wheel.

The police siren, it turned out, was for us.

"Pull over," Yannick told Margaret. "Pull over, Margaret. Pull the fuck over."

He was scared, too. Margaret blinked. I hoped that did not impede her ability to see the road.

"I am trying," she said. "I have to slow down first. I can't just slam to a stop. And I need to find a way to pull over. There are other cars on the road. I can't just pull over."

We were in the left lane, cleared of cars, as if an entire highway had gotten out of the way of Judy's red car. Margaret signaled and she angled the car into the middle lane. And then signaled again into the right, and then, finally pulled over onto the shoulder. The police car was right behind us, bright lights flashing.

The officer asked for license and registration, just like in the movies. "Okay," Margaret said. "I am sorry."

Margaret was crying. Fortunately, she had her license. She gave that to the officer and her campus ID.

"This I don't need," he said, kindly. "Just the registration."

I did not know if I had the registration. I was not sure if I could prove that I owned the car. I was waiting for Judy, wanting her to say something for herself. Because I did not believe that Margaret would drive like that on her own. Which meant what? That the spirit of my dead boss had entered her body and put her foot on the gas?

"Check the glove compartment," I told Yannick.

It was right where it was supposed to be, the registration and also Judy's insurance papers.

"This car belong to you?" he asked Margaret.

"Me," I said from the back. "It belongs to me. My friend died and she left it to me in her will."

"Stay in the car," he said. "I am going to run these."

"Holy shit," Yannick said.

"I'm sorry," I said.

"Why are you sorry?" Margaret snapped. "I was the one who was driving. I want to get out of this car. Do you think I can get out?"

"I think we should wait," I said. "I don't think police like sudden movement."

"Margaret is a white girl from Stanford," Yannick said. "She can get out of the car."

"I don't think you should," I said.

The police officer returned.

"You are going to have to get this automobile registered in your name, miss," he told me.

I nodded.

He wrote out a ticket to Margaret.

"I am sorry, officer," Margaret said.

"Wait until you see the ticket," he said.

"A lot?" Margaret asked.

"You were going considerably over the speed limit."

"I felt some strange feeling come over me," she said.

It was the wrong thing to say.

"I am going to have to ask you to step out of the car," the police officer said.

"Can we get out, too?" I asked him.

There was something scary about sitting in a parked car on the shoulder of the road. The car shook every time a truck passed. I thought the police officer would say no, but he looked at us, me and Yannick, and said, "Go ahead."

Actually it was surprising that he hadn't asked before. He was not done with us. He asked Margaret to walk in a straight line, which she wasn't quite able to do.

"I feel a little bit wobbly," she said. "I am so nervous. I am not drunk. I swear."

"You're fine, Margaret," Yannick called.

"Can he hold my hand?"

"Got to do it yourself, sweetheart," the officer said.

Margaret tried again and she was able to walk in a straight line. The police officer then gave her a Breathalyzer test, which she also passed.

"I would never drink and drive," she said.

"Good thing," he said. "I have a feeling you are going to think twice again about speeding."

Margaret nodded. Yannick came over to her side and held her hand. I liked him again, how sweet he was. He didn't say, What were you thinking, driving so fast? He just held her hand.

"I don't think I can drive home," Margaret told the police officer.

He looked at us.

"I don't have a driver's license," Yannick said.

The police officer looked at me.

I shook my head.

We stood there. I thought maybe we would have to get the red car towed. I would pay for it. I wondered what that cost. I wondered what I was thinking, driving the car to Palo Alto. But I hadn't sped. I had not gotten pulled over. I had driven under the speed limit, annoying other cars on the road, constantly passed, but safe.

The police officer had a partner.

"Get in the police car. We'll take you home."

The three of us squished in together in the backseat, behind the police grate, as if we had been arrested, but we had not been arrested, only ticketed, and this drive home was an act of kindness. We did not speak. The police officer did not know that Yannick was a genius, only that he had dark skin and dreadlocks. But they treated us okay, all of us. The police officer drove us to back to Margaret's house and the other officer drove Judy's red car, parking it back in the street where we started.

"I might have to throw up," Margaret said.

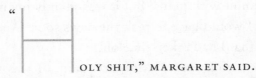

"HOLY SHIT," MARGARET SAID.

I had changed out of my black dress, into a pair of black leggings and my kitten T-shirt. Yannick brought out a bottle of wine. Margaret sat cross-legged on the couch, studying the speeding ticket. It was in the amount of $540.00 and it would also be reported to her insurance company, which would probably increase the cost of her policy. "Fuck," Margaret said.

Until today, I had never heard Margaret curse.

"I am sorry," I said. "That is a lot of money."

There was something about the way her voice caught. In college, Margaret had worked as a maid off campus. Haverford was set in an affluent area and house cleaning paid more than double the student jobs, but I remember being surprised she had been willing to do that kind of work. Summers, she had been a waitress at the International House of Pancakes, a wretched job according to her. Margaret paid her way. She worked hard. It was easy to forget this, living in a fancy house, even if it wasn't properly furnished. She had her Stanford job, her future seemingly assured.

"This was not your fault," Margaret said.

Of course, it was my fault. I was the one who had brought the red car into her life.

"I could pay it," I said. "Your ticket."

Judy had said that she had left me money in that letter she wrote. Eventually, I would have to go back to the office where I once worked, talk to Beverly. There was an envelope waiting for me. A painting. Regardless, I had money of my own, in a joint account with Hans. But it was mainly my money. I realized that I would have to pick the news soon. And then I remembered that I had taken time off.

"Of course, you won't," Margaret said. "I was the one behind the wheel."

"We could split it," I said.

"I want something to eat," Yannick said. "I will be right back."

"There's cheese," Margaret said. "And olives."

"That is not what I am in the mood for," Yannick said. "I'll come back with something."

We watched him disappear into the kitchen.

Wouldn't it be funny, I thought, if he never came back. "He hates conversations about money," Margaret said, as if reading my mind. "It's childish. He can talk about sex. He can talk about any anthropological concept, or Derrida, feminist theory, but when we discuss expenses, he gets downright fidgety."

There was a back door to the house in the kitchen. Yannick could simply open it and disappear. That would also be my fault. I imagined myself apologizing to Margaret, but what was there that I could say? Instead, he returned with a tray of brownies. I was so happy to see Yannick. The relief I felt was enormous. It didn't even matter that he had somehow brought out the very brownies I had eaten that morning.

"I thought I finished them," I said. "While you were sleeping. I was going to tell you."

"I noticed that," Margaret said, wagging her finger at me.

"These came from the freezer," Yannick said.

"I always keep a back-up tray," Margaret said.

"In case of emergencies," Yannick said.

They were rock hard, too hard to cut.

"The microwave, sweetheart," Margaret said.

Yannick got right up and went back into the kitchen. I heard the beep beep beep of the microwave. Of course he didn't disappear. I wondered why I would think that.

"It is amazing how much he's changed," I said.

"I know," Margaret said. "After we slept together, this was about six months ago, I thought it was going to be like the last time. Remember?" I remembered. This was many years ago, when she had first started at Stanford. She had pretended it did not mean anything, but really she was heartbroken. "And this time, I wasn't okay with it, and I told him that. I told him I wanted to be in a committed relationship and I wouldn't have sex with him ever again unless he agreed. I never thought he would say okay."

"From what I can see," I said, "he seems completely committed to you."

Margaret smiled. "Doesn't he? This is just a speeding ticket." Margaret sighed. "It could have been much worse."

I told Margaret, then, finally, about how I had gotten the red car, how Judy had died in the car, how she may or may not have committed suicide in it, how the car had magically restored itself.

"I shouldn't have let you drive it," I said.

"It is such a beautiful car," Margaret said. "I would have wanted to drive it anyway."

"You seem so different," I said.

"I know. I feel different. I feel good. I am not the same person you met at college. I used to be such a mouse. I look at pictures of myself from back then and I wince."

"I wish I could change like that."

"Of course you can," Margaret said. "Why couldn't you? Haven't you already? You are always doing something interesting. Here you are. What is going on with you? We haven't talked in ages. I haven't asked you about Gerhardt."

"Hans," I said.

"Hans," Margaret repeated. "I can't believe I said that. I have this German student in my class. He sits in the front row in these perfectly pressed clothes and takes notes. I find him unnerving. How is Hans?"

I hugged my knees. Why did it feel like my life had stopped once I had gotten married? Earlier that same day, it felt like a very long time ago, I had sat on that same couch and read my novel. Even though I was editing, deleting sentences, adding commas, removing commas, it felt like I was reading a book someone else had written. Sitting in the backseat of Judy's red car, as Margaret drove faster and faster, I realized that I was afraid of dying. It would not have surprised me if Margaret had driven straight into the back of a truck and that would have been it, for all of us. I did not want to die.

It was a good thing to know.

I did not want to talk about Gerhardt. Or Hans. I did not want to think about going home. I liked Margaret's couch. It was purple. It was comfortable. I wondered if Margaret had bought this couch or if Stella had left it behind. It felt familiar.

Yannick came back with the brownies and a bottle of

whiskey and three glasses; it was a well-done balancing act. "I think this goes better with the chocolate," he said. We had not touched the wine.

"Absolutely." Margaret smiled.

"I was afraid we were going to die," I said.

"Me, too," Margaret said.

"I can't believe the police drove us home like that," Yannick said. "It absolutely ruins my sense of righteous indignation about police brutality."

"Thank god," Margaret said.

"I do go to Stanford," Yannick said.

"That doesn't always make a difference."

"And I am light skinned."

"It would have been my fault," I said.

"Like you had your foot on the gas petal," Yannick said. "Did I hear that the car is haunted?"

"I don't ordinarily believe in such things," I said. "But yes. Maybe. I think so."

"Margaret seemed possessed."

"I don't know," Margaret said. "I just wanted to drive faster and faster and then, when I realized I should slow down, I didn't know how. It was like the car wouldn't let me. Like there was an invisible force field on my foot."

Yannick burst out laughing. But I listened seriously, wondering what it meant, knowing it was true. Judy wrote that she loved me. If she loved me, that had to further imply that she didn't want to kill me. That she didn't want to kill my friends. Did she have control of her car? Maybe her car had knowingly killed her, acting upon her wishes. What if Judy had wanted to change her mind? I remembered what the mechanic had told me: The car had fixed itself.

I felt cold, an unnatural chill. I ate a bite of partially frozen brownie. It melted in my mouth. It seemed like the right way to live, having an emergency tray of brownies in the freezer. It also felt right to be in this living room, with these friends. I felt lucky.

"Can I keep my kitten shirt?" I asked.

"Duh," Yannick said.

He poured a glass of whiskey to go with my brownie. He filled three glasses.

"You have to get rid of that car," Margaret said.

"Maybe you should write a paper about it first," Yannick said.

Margaret nodded.

"I have to get serious about writing again," she said.

That sounded more like the Margaret I knew. The subject had changed and I never had to answer a question about myself, my marriage. I was glad about that. I held my glass of whiskey with both hands, admiring the refection of the gold liquid in the light.

WE WERE DRUNK WHEN THE doorbell rang.

"Wrong number," Yannick said.

This made sense. Except it was not the telephone.

"I am not expecting anybody," Margaret said.

"Don't answer," Yannick said.

We didn't. Immediately, it was quiet again. It was quiet in Palo Alto.

"We totally imagined it," Margaret said, laughing.

"All of us," Yannick said, "had a simultaneous sensory impression."

"What did you put in the whiskey?" Margaret asked.

"Margaret was so straight when we were in college," I told Yannick.

"Everyone was," Margaret said.

"Not me," I said.

"You were a mystery," Margaret said.

"I made sure I threw up before my freshman year."

"Ahead of the curve," Yannick said.

The doorbell rang again.

"What time is it?" Margaret said.

I expected it to be the middle of the night. I looked down at my wrist. I was wearing a watch. It was an expensive watch, a man's watch with a rectangular face and roman numerals, a leather band. It had been a wedding gift from my mother to Hans. She had given us matching watches. I had lost mine but Hans never wore his. It turned out I liked his better anyway and so I wore it. I stared at the watch. I loved this watch. The doorbell rang again. I realized I was looking at the watch because I wanted to know what time it was. I focused on the roman numerals. It was only ten o'clock.

I wondered how Hans had found me here. I had not told him I was going to Palo Alto. I had not returned any of his most recent emails. I knew that I should, but I could not think of what to say. Of course, he would be worried about me, but he could not actually be here. That was impossible. He would have had to get on an airplane.

"People take airplanes all the time," Judy said.

"Shit," I said.

It happened again, the doorbell. I started to cry.

"It's just the doorbell," Yannick said. He scooted over to me on the couch and held my hand. "You don't have to cry."

"I will get the door," Margaret said, looking at me, worry on her face.

"I wouldn't do that," Yannick said.

"You barely answer the phone," Margaret said.

"I have enough trouble with my email," Yannick said.

"Me, too," I said.

The doorbell rang again.

It was the fifth time.

"Coming," Margaret said, heading to the door.

"Who do you think it is?" I asked Yannick.

"Jehovah's Witness?" he said. "Neighbors complaining about the noise."

But the music was turned on low.

It wasn't possible that Hans could be there, even if people did take airplanes. He did not like to make decisions without consulting with me first. He did not know that I was in Palo Alto. I sat up straight, wiped the tears from my face with the bottom of my kitten T-shirt. I would want to wash it in the morning. I had a tendency to ruin my clothes. I did not want to ruin this shirt. I wondered if I could take another one. There was a whole box.

I closed my eyes, expecting a snide comment from Judy. But there was nothing. I felt good with my eyes closed. I could hear Margaret talking to someone in the front of the house. Another graduate student, I thought, no big mystery, maybe the person who provided the psychedelic mushrooms the night before. Someone who came for the brownies. Probably she was notorious in the department, not just for her intellect but her baking. Maybe this is what made the difference for Yannick, made him think, *Yes, I will commit to this woman. Brownies*. I kept my eyes shut tight, the way I used to when I was a kid, when I used to rub them so hard that I could see a show of fireworks beneath my eyelids, purples and pinks and yellows. I prayed that it wasn't Hans. Please don't be Hans.

The room was much too quiet.

I opened my eyes and Jonathan Beene was standing in front of me. So I had been partially right. It was a man, looking for me.

"Leah," he said. He actually sank down on his knees so that we were eye level. "Do you know how often I think about you?"

I shook my head.

"I don't know," I said. There were still tears in my eyes. It did not make sense, how afraid I was. "I have no idea how often you think about me."

"All the time. Several times a week. Maybe once a day. Before I go to sleep."

"What do you think?" I asked.

Jonathan Beene blushed.

He did not answer.

"You don't actually think about me," I said.

But of course he did. He had just said so. Why would he say it if it wasn't true? And there he was in Margaret's living room.

I remembered now. We had planned on going to his reception after the lecture. Or Margaret and Yannick were going to go to the reception. Then Margaret had gotten pulled over for speeding and we had forgotten all about it.

"Can I have a drink, please?" Jonathan asked.

It was funny having him there on his knees in front of me. Like a marriage proposal. I could not remember how Hans and I decided to get married. There wasn't a moment. There was a realization. He would have to leave the country if we did not marry. His student visa was expiring. Honestly, I had never been a big fan of marriage. I had my parents' marriage as an example, my mother bitter and unfulfilled, my father uncomprehending of my mother, bored. He wanted to drive to Atlantic City and play blackjack. My mother loathed Atlantic City. They were not the right people for each other. They had been married forty years.

It had been such a long time since I had last seen Jonathan Beene. I hadn't actually been kicked out of college. I probably wouldn't have been. There had been some kind of joint mediation scheduled, an appointment with a counselor. It was much easier to leave. I had packed my two suitcases and walked to the train station. I had not said good-bye to anyone. I walked down the long driveway that led me away from the college, past the idyllic duck pond, past the Wawa, to the train station. I took the train home. I had let myself in the front door of my parents' house. My timing had been good. My mother had made meatballs and spaghetti for dinner.

Yannick poured Jonathan a whiskey.

I had no words for Jonathan Beene. I was still just so grateful that he was not Hans. And what did that tell me? My profound gratitude that the man at the door was not Hans. Jonathan Beene got up off his knees. He sat in an armchair in his blazer and white shirt with his whiskey. We were all grown-ups. Margaret told him about the speeding ticket.

"I have a red car," I said. "A sports car."

It felt impolite not to talk at all.

Jonathan Beene tilted his head to the side, like a confused dog. "I didn't notice it," he said.

We all went outside to look at Judy's car. I could swear that the door, the door where another car had crashed into Judy, killing her, had begun caving inward. I remembered the day when Judy first showed the car to me, in the parking lot of our office building, pretty much demanding that I admire it. We had gone out for tapas. We drank sangria. We had made a toast, to our future good fortune.

"That doesn't look like a car you would drive," Jonathan said. Which made me wonder, how would he know what kind of car I would drive? And why had he reported us to the honor board. Jesus. I had not gotten over that. What kind of fucking idiot would do that?

"What kind of car do you drive?" I asked.

"Subaru," he said.

Yannick laughed. "I thought you would say Prius," he said.

"They were sold out. Waiting list was a year long. Subarus are energy efficient and reliable. I don't require an ostentatious car."

It was so quiet in the suburbs of Palo Alto. Almost as if we were in the woods. I could see the flickering lights of a TV inside the house across the street. The sky was black, full of stars. A skinny sliver of a moon. The air felt good, crisp and clean. Summer was better in California. I heard the voice of Hans, telling me what a shithole it was in Queens, where we lived. But I sort of liked it there. I liked the Mexican restaurant where we ate tacos. I liked the subway station at Steinway Street, I even liked waiting for the train. But there were never any stars.

It was a gorgeous night. Jonathan Beene stood next me. We were the same height. He smelled nice. Was it possible? He smelled like college.

WE SAT ON THE STEPS of Margaret's house, looking at the stars. Just me and Jonathan Beene.

"Where do you live?" I asked finally.

"New York," he said. "How about you?"

"Me, too," I said. "What neighborhood are you in?"

"Tribeca," he said. "I have a loft. What about you?"

"Astoria," I said. "I rent an apartment."

"I went to Astoria once," he said.

"You went to a Greek restaurant," I said.

"How did you know?"

I shrugged.

I met them all the time, people from Manhattan, proud of themselves for taking the train into Queens to eat at a Greek restaurant. I rarely went to Greek restaurants. They were expensive, they did not thrill me. Margaret and Yannick had gone back inside. It seemed on purpose, a decision to leave us alone. But I did not want to be left alone with Jonathan Beene. That was not why I came to Palo Alto. I didn't know why I had come to Palo Alto.

"So you don't know what you want," Judy said.

This seemed like one of her lamer observations.

"I am normally a very articulate person," Jonathan Beene

said. "I frequently speak in front of large groups of people. What I say matters."

I nodded. It made sense, that success would make you arrogant. I would like that for myself, a degree of arrogance.

"You broke a water glass," I observed. "That was pretty smooth."

"That happened because I saw you," he said.

"I read about you," I told him. "Maybe a year ago, in *The New York Times*."

"You read that article?"

"I was at my parents' house," I said. "I was eating a bagel with cream cheese." I wondered why I added that detail.

"You read it," he repeated.

"I did."

"You didn't call me."

I turned my head to look at Jonathan Beene, to see if he was serious. It seemed like such a strange thing to say.

"The article didn't list your phone number," I said. Though that wasn't an honest answer. "I guess it never occurred to me to call you," I said, slowly. "I was happy for you. I remember thinking to myself, Wow, you are successful."

This, of course, would be a reason not to call him.

"I always wanted to be your boyfriend," he said.

"I knew that."

"You really hurt me," he said.

I stretched out my arms, lacing my fingers together, and then setting them back down on my lap. There I was, having this conversation with Jonathan Beene. "You really hurt me, too," I said.

"I'm sorry," he said.

He took my hand.

I observed my hand, my fingers now interlaced with Jonathan's. I took it back. "That was a long time ago," I said.

"I guess so."

"Anyway, it's like you said. You are a major success and I am a nobody. So, it all worked out."

"No," Judy and Jonathan said, simultaneously.

I laughed. They seemed to cancel each other out. No response seemed necessary.

"I would take it back now," Jonathan said.

"Which part?" I said. "The sex or the honor council?"

"The honor council. Jesus. What a fucking idiot. I would take back the honor council. The sex was like the best thing that ever happened to me. You blew my mind. The honor council. My god. I just wanted you to love me and you didn't. You wanted money," he said. "It made me crazy."

"It was just a game," I said.

"I was so mad. Because you were playing with me. But I didn't realize how lucky I was."

"No one had sex at Haverford College," I said.

"I still want to apologize to you."

"All these years later," I said.

"I am sorry, Leah. Really sorry."

I felt something in me loosen, break apart almost. It made me feel so happy to hear the exact words I wanted to hear. The moment was something I would have written if I could have, it felt so perfect. Only I hadn't known how much I wanted it. I thought I had forgotten about him.

"Thank you," I said.

"You are welcome," he said.

I felt the grin spread across my face, from ear to ear. Like a Cheshire cat. I started to laugh. Jonathan Beene gazed back at me. "Why are you laughing?" he said.

There, in front of me, was Judy's red car, the car that had killed her. I did not know what I was supposed to do about that.

"I feel happy," I said.

I took his hand, our fingers interlaced.

"You were never happy in college," he said.

Jonathan Beene was smiling, smiling at me.

That was the thing, I was starting to realize. I liked it, being happy.

DIDN'T KNOW WHAT I WAS supposed to do next.

"Huh, Judy?" I said.

It was the middle of the night. Jonathan Beene was asleep in what was supposed to be my bedroom, Stella's old room. He had wanted to sleep with me. I had said no. "I am married," I said.

"You are?"

I appreciated the disappointment on his face. I appreciated how being married made this conversation easy for me. I did not have to hurt his feelings. I did not tell Jonathan about Diego or the other Lea. He didn't need to know. I wondered what my life would be like, if I were to have sex with Jonathan Beene. Maybe I would be able to go back with him to his loft in Tribeca. My life would be significantly better. Somehow, that seemed wrong. Like prostitution. I also did not want to have sex with him. I was tired.

Instead, I found a blanket, a pillow, and settled in on the couch. I wanted to sleep but I couldn't sleep. I read Judy's letter again. There was the part about money, how she had left me money. I wanted the money. I did not know how to kick Hans out of my apartment, our apartment, because he would have nowhere to go. The easiest solution seemed like leaving.

"That's running," Judy said.

But I didn't want to live in that apartment anymore. Some-how, I had lived there for five years. Five years had passed. For five years, I had lived in an apartment on an ugly block with an auto repair shop on the corner, constantly tormented by the noise made in that shop. This summer, it had been the swim-ming pool in the yard, making me feel crazy. I wanted out.

"Not running," I said. Or maybe it was running. "So what?" I said.

I had always admired people who went running. Runners. People who ran marathons. People who could run two miles. Even that seemed impossible. They seemed like better people than I was.

"I am not judging," Judy said.

But she had been judging me all along.

Her letter also asked me to go the bat mitzvah of her niece in Philadelphia. The date was coming up. "Philadelphia?" I said. "Really?"

I fell asleep with the letter on my lap, my contact lenses still in. I woke up to Margaret sitting next to me, bright light streaming in from the windows. Margaret was wearing her professor clothes, her hair pulled back.

She had put a cup of coffee on the coffee table for me. "Jona-than already left," she said. "He wrote you a letter." I saw the piece of paper, folded in half, next to my cup of coffee. "You can stay as long as you want," she said. "I have to teach."

Yannick came out of the kitchen, carrying a bowl of cereal. He sat in the armchair. I liked it, this sense of camaraderie in their living room. It seemed like an episode of *Friends*. It had never felt this good before, living with roommates. Living with Hans.

"Did you get lucky?" Yannick asked.

"That is disgusting," Margaret said. "And you know they slept in different rooms."

I carefully picked up my cup of coffee. Margaret had filled the mug to the rim.

"He is worth a lot of money," Yannick said.

"That seems like a strange thing for an anthropologist to say," I said. I sipped my coffee. It was good coffee. Strong. I could stay there, in Margaret's house, she had said so. It was an appealing idea. Our life could be a sitcom. I would play the role of the wacky friend who came to visit and never left.

"Anthropologists have to get by in this world," Yannick said. "We can't live on grant money alone."

"Well, maybe you can," Margaret said.

Yannick shrugged.

"I am going to have to wing today's lecture," Margaret said. "I hate that. I drank too much last night. Again."

"Did you take any aspirin?" Yannick asked.

"Two," Margaret said. "My body is not forgiving me. I think I am going to make the students write in class."

"I'm sorry," I said.

I was just waking up, but it didn't seem like I had a hangover. I felt great, somehow, fresh, clear.

"You don't have to be sorry," Margaret said.

"But it is my fault," I said.

"I am not going to drink for a month," Margaret said.

"Or until dinner," Yannick said.

I looked at Margaret.

"We do drink wine with dinner," she said. "But I don't get drunk. I won't. I have too much work to do."

I thought about dinner. Margaret was a vegetarian. She used to make nice pastas. There was always cheese. The wine. The brownies. But I could not stay there, in her house. She had work to do. She had made a life for herself. It was a nice life. I envied it. I wondered what Jonathan Beene had written to me in his letter.

"Another letter," Judy said.

Which was better than whatever was waiting for me in my email.

"I am sorry you are behind," I told Margaret again.

Margaret shook her head. "I am a grown-up," she said. "I make my own choices. We had fun."

"I should go, too," I said. "I don't want to."

"You don't have to go."

"I do," I said. "I have things I need to do. You have been the greatest."

"Sweetie," Margaret said.

I got up from the couch. Margaret gave me the biggest, most wonderful hug.

"You are going to be okay," she said.

PUT THE KEYS IN JUDY'S red car.

"Please don't kill me," I said.

The obvious place to go was back to Diego's condo in San Francisco. But when I got on the highway, I realized that I had taken the wrong ramp, going south instead of north. There was a large concrete divider in between the lanes. I felt a strange urge, as if coming from the red car, to go ahead and jump it. And I didn't know why the red car would try to kill me, why Judy would send me out on this path if she was also trying to kill me.

The thing to do was take the first exit, make a safe and legal U-turn, head back in the right direction, but I was in the middle lane, driving five miles over the speed limit the way my father once taught me. I was not speeding like Margaret. I was not going too slow. I was in control of the red car. I did not feel like I was in control of the red car. My hands were gripping the steering wheel, much too tight. I looked at my bent knuckles on my hands and realized I should be looking at the road. There were cars behind me, in front of me, on my left, on my right. I should not have been driving this red car on a crowded highway. I drove for over an hour, safe in the middle lane, willing myself to switch lanes. I no longer knew where I was going. It did not seem to matter. I pictured the hippie mechanic, picking up the car at a junkyard, shaking his head, wishing it would have worked out differently. He would have sold it for me. We would have slept together. It would not have been terrible sex. I would not be dead.

"You are not dead, dummy," Judy said.

"Thanks, Judy," I said.

"You'll see," she answered.

"See what?" I said.

I saw a turnoff to Highway 1.

I was able to make it.

Something in my brain clicked. I knew this was a beautiful road, famous, but the choice turned out to be a bad one. Maybe the scenery was gorgeous but I couldn't turn my head to look, because I had to concentrate on the twists and turns of the road, all too aware of another car on my tail. It was a narrow highway.

"Fuck off," I said.

I wanted to pull over to let the car pass me but I was too scared to pull over. I could not see the ocean, but I knew that it was there, at the bottom of the cliffs. I could imagine missing a turn, sailing off the road into the unknown like the black funeral car in *Harold and Maude*.

My knuckles hurt. I was sitting up way too straight. My back hurt. It had never hurt before. I did not want to have a bad back. Hans's back always, always hurt. A year ago, he had injured himself during a yoga class and I had not been sympathetic. I couldn't explain why. He wasn't easy to take care of when he was sick.

I did not know where was I driving but I wanted to be done driving. It was a beautiful day, but the glare of the sun shone straight into my eyes, and I was blinking. Driving straight into the sun, I felt almost blind. I was driving blind on a twisty road in a red car with murderous impulses. The combination was bad. If this were a Haruki Murakami novel, at least I would be listening to the right music, a Beach Boys cassette or some old jazz, but I was too scared to take my hand off the wheel to turn on the radio.

I saw a sign for a motel and I felt another click in my brain. The River Inn. My parents had gone there together, a long time ago. I could not remember the last time my parents had been on vacation, but I knew that they had been there. My mother loved this place. She had told me about wooden benches in the river, which in places was more like a gentle stream. You could sit on these benches, read a book, drink a lemonade and dangle your feet in the water. I still had a picture of my mother that she sent me, years ago, her hair long, wearing a magenta T-shirt and a pair of shorts, sitting on one of these wooden benches in the river at the River Inn, her feet in the water. It was one of the rare pictures of my mother, who did not like to be photographed. It was one of the rare times that she was smiling.

I pulled into the driveway, the car crunching over a gravel path. The place did not look like much. It looked like a motel on the side of the road, nothing more. I went into the office, which was empty, and rang the bell. My hands were wet with sweat from gripping the steering wheel.

A young Asian woman appeared from the back, rubbing her eyes. She had the straightest, blackest hair. The whitest skin. I thought of Snow White. She was almost too beautiful for this world. She was holding an F. Scott Fitzgerald novel. She was wearing a pale pink sweatshirt.

"Sorry," she said. "I must have fallen asleep."

"That's okay," I said.

"Do you have a reservation?" she asked.

I shook my head, sure that she would send me away. I felt disappointed, suddenly wanting to stay in this place where my mother had been happy. I did not want to be sent away.

"Have some faith," Judy said.

The beautiful Asian girl squinted at the computer screen.

"That's okay," she said. "There are a couple of rooms open. How many nights?"

"One," I said and then I paused. "Could I stay longer if I like it?"

"Oh, you will like it here," she said.

Her straight hair formed a blanket in front of her face. I could not see her eyes. "Let's start with one night and you can extend if you want to. Does that sound okay?"

That sounded reasonable to me.

"Thank you," I said.

"Cash or credit?"

Without thinking, I gave her my credit card. She pushed her hair behind her ears and I watched her begin to enter my information into the computer. And then it occurred to me, watching her, that Hans could find out where I was. He could call the credit card company, research my expenses. There was no reason for him to do that. That was what a husband would do when his wife went missing. Like the Julia Roberts movie that was always on cable, when she was still really young, where she cut off her hair and learned to swim, pretended to drown, swam to shore and went on to lead a new life in a small bucolic American town. All to escape her controlling, abusive husband.

But I was not missing. I was not even on the run. I had a plane ticket, a return date. Maybe I was on a break? Was that what it was? Hans and I had not discussed it. I had not explained to him, for instance, that I did not want to talk to him while I was gone. How could he be expected to understand that?

"Actually, could I pay cash?" I asked.

"Of course," the beautiful receptionist said. "I will still need to take down the information from your card, though," she said. "For a security deposit. Just in case. I will also need a form of ID. I should have asked for that straightaway. I am a little bit tired. I was up all night, reading this book. Have you read it?"

She held up her copy of *Tender Is the Night*.

"Sure, I read it," I said. "A long time ago."

"It's really good," the receptionist said.

I opened my wallet and extracted a pile of twenties, the money Hans had considerately taken from the ATM after choking me. I instinctively reached for my neck, patted the soft skin and then my hair. I envied the hair of the receptionist. It felt good to have so much money in my wallet, but the room was more expensive than what I thought a motel on the side of the highway would cost. It would not last long. I could hear my mother the last time I was home, complaining about the rising price of produce in the supermarket. I wondered if the River Inn cost significantly less when she had come. If that was why she no longer took trips.

"Don't worry about money," Judy said. "I told you that. Can you trust me?"

I did not know. Could I trust her? She had left me money. I just had to go and claim it. But I did not want to go back to San Francisco.

"Stay," Judy said. "You are fine."

"My mother stayed here once," I told the beautiful receptionist. "She loved it. I was driving by and I saw the sign for this place and so I pulled over. Completely on impulse. I had absolutely no idea that I would come here."

I regretted talking too much. I was nervous, I realized, checking into a motel where no one knew where I was. Where Hans did not know where I was. I didn't like to remember that fight. Hans's hands around my neck. I did not want to think about him. I didn't want to have to answer his emails, pretend that everything was all right.

"You'll see after you check in," the beautiful receptionist said, handwriting me a receipt she'd made using a black quill pen, dipped in ink. Surely, a ballpoint pen would be quicker, a computer receipt. I looked at her pretty hair and wondered how she came to be working here. Maybe she was an actress, training for a role. "It's really spectacular here. Check into your room and come for brunch. You'll see the view."

"Okay," I said.

The receptionist squinted at the computer screen. I thought we were done, but the information was not going through.

"I didn't fill in a required field," she said. "I need to enter the make of your car and your license plate."

"I don't know it," I said. "Let me go check."

"Okay. I'll go with you," the receptionist said. "I need some air."

By now, I knew that I wanted this beautiful Asian receptionist to be my friend.

"Is this yours?" she asked, pointing at Judy's red car.

"It was a gift," I said.

"It isn't what I would have expected you to be driving."

The receptionist wrote my license plate number down on
the back of her hand. It struck me as funny, like Lea from the
apartment on Castro Street giving me her phone number. I
looked down at the skin on my wrist. Her number was gone.
It didn't matter. I knew where she lived. The beautiful receptionist walked me to my room. If she had been a man, I might
have found this creepy. Instead, I was grateful. My room was
in a flat, unremarkable one-story building on the other side of
the two-lane highway.

"Come straight to the restaurant," she said. "The kitchen
is going to close soon."

"Brunch," I said.

"Coffee," the receptionist said, kindly, as if I did not understand the word. "Eggs. Toast. Homemade granola. French toast."

"Pancakes?" I asked her. I could not remember the last time
I had eaten a pancake.

"Delicious pancakes," she said. "With fresh fruit and
organic maple syrup."

I opened the door to my motel room. Again, it did not look
like much. There was wood paneling on the walls, a framed
photograph of sunflowers over the double bed. An armchair in
the corner, a door that would open up to a bathroom.

"The restaurant is across the highway. There are outdoor
tables that look out onto the river."

"That's nice."

"You have half an hour before the kitchen closes."

I stepped inside my room. Maybe I liked it after all. The place was mine. I did not have to share it with anyone else. I was worried that my new receptionist friend would follow me into my room.

She left.

THE MENU HAD TOO MANY choices. Six differ-
ent kinds of toast. Omelets with goat cheese and varieties of
mushrooms I had never heard of. I chose a table outside on the
patio with a view of the river. It was beautiful. I ordered the
pancakes because the Asian receptionist had told me she loved
the pancakes. I asked for coffee.

There I was.

I did not understand how, geographically, there could be
a river at Big Sur because I thought I was by the ocean. But
the receptionist was right. I did love it there. It was like I had
crossed the highway and been transported to another world.
Blue sky. Tall grass. Wildflowers. Ducks. A mother duck with
baby ducklings in the river, which was actually more like
a bubbling brook. I could hear the pleasant tinkling of the
water. I waited for my food, elbows on the table, my head on
my hands, watching the water flow over the rocks. I looked
out onto the wooden benches in the water, the benches my
mother had loved, where she had let her picture be taken.
My coffee came.

"Thank you," I said.

I wasn't going to look at the waiter who took my order,
but I felt a lingering presence. My pretty receptionist friend

set down a red mug on the table, a small pitcher of cream. I noticed another red ceramic mug, also filled with coffee, on the tray. The patio was empty. I tried to remember what day it was.

"Are you the waitress, too?" I asked her.

"No," she said. "I saw you come in and I decided to bring your coffee."

"I don't know your name," I said, motioning for her to sit. She smiled. The other coffee was for her. She sat down and poured cream into her cup. I did the same.

"It's Yumiko," she said.

"That is so pretty," I said.

I worried if that was a racist thing to say. To compliment her Japanese name. Maybe in Japan it was an ordinary name.

"It means snow," Yumiko said.

"I didn't know that," I said.

"Why would you?" she said, smiling at me. She had pulled her pretty hair back into a ponytail. "You are not Japanese."

I almost said that I liked sushi. I felt strangely nervous. Instead I mentioned a famous Japanese writer whose work that I loved. I was not sure why. Was it as if to say that I liked Japanese people? It was almost as bad as telling a black person that you had a black friend.

"That is my uncle," Yumiko said nonchalantly, sipping her coffee.

"Who?"

"The writer you love."

"You are kidding me," I said.

"He is teaching this year at the writing program down

at Irvine," she said. "I dropped out of college in Tokyo, my parents were worried about me, so he suggested I come down to California with him and study there, but I dropped out again."

"And you came here?"

"I have been here for two months. I don't want to leave. I was about to run out of money but I asked for a job."

The real waiter returned with my pancakes.

"Hey, Yumiko," he said.

It was clear to me, right away, that the waiter was in love with her. It made sense. I was a little bit in love with her. Three round pancakes were served on a blue ceramic plate, a beautiful fruit salad in a hole carved in the center. Looking at these perfect pancakes, I realized that I wasn't in the mood for pancakes. I had ordered them because they were what Yumiko had recommended. They were not what I wanted.

"Would you want some?" I asked Yumiko.

She nodded.

"I'll bring another plate," the waiter said.

"Could I also have some buttered toast?" I asked. "And two poached eggs."

That was what I actually wanted for breakfast.

"What kind of bread?" the waiter asked.

There were six different kinds of bread. I asked for sourdough. "The sourdough bread is really good," Yumiko said.

We sat in companionable silence, Yumiko eating the pancakes. We both looked out at the view. There was something about the light reflecting off the river. The waiter returned with my new breakfast, moving the plate of pancakes in front of Yumiko. I wondered if this was something she did periodically. The waiter refilled our coffee.

"Can I join you guys?" he asked.

Yumiko shook her head.

I thought this was funny, after she joined me at my table. I was glad, though, that she sent him away.

"It's going to be time for me to leave here soon," Yumiko told me. "I am starting to get restless, honestly. Everywhere I go, men fall in love with me. It is such a pain."

I was almost going to say that I had no idea what that was like, men always falling in love with me, and then I remembered Jonathan Beene and Hans and the stream of emails that would be waiting for me. Perhaps men were always falling in love with me, too, but they weren't men that I wanted. The last man I wanted, Diego, he did not want me.

"Diego is sweet. He's good-looking," Judy said. "But he is not the man for you."

Sitting with Yumiko, I had almost forgotten about Judy. She was still around. That was okay, almost reassuring, since she had gotten me here in the first place. "Shitty place to be, huh," Judy said.

I did not remember her to be so acerbic in real life. But I had been gone for a while. Or I had a vivid imagination.

I drank more coffee, grateful for this coffee. I also felt shy around Yumiko. She preferred me to the waiter, but that did not necessarily mean much. I had a feeling that she did not mind silence, that she had no problem saying what she wanted. She had finished the pancakes, eating everything on the plate but one piece of overripe strawberry.

"I can't stay here that much longer anyway," Yumiko said. "I think I stayed here as long as I did to meet you."

I looked at Yumiko. Her shiny ponytail. Her pink sweatshirt. It took me by surprise, again, how lovely she was.

"That is so nice," I said.

"It's true," Yumiko said. "And thank you for the pancakes."

"I am glad you liked them."

"I think it's time for me to travel. Maybe go to San Francisco. Portland, Seattle. My student visa will end in August. So when my uncle leaves, I go, too."

"That's why I got married," I said.

Yumiko looked at me, surprised.

"You're married?" she said.

It was the first time she seemed surprised about anything.

"His visa was about to expire," I explained. "My husband. He's from Austria."

I looked at her.

"I don't like Austrians," she said. "Germans either. I don't like their glasses. I don't like their work ethic. They remind me of the Japanese."

"Ha," I said.

"Did you want to get married?" Yumiko asked me.

"Not really," I said, surprised by my honesty. This did not seem like something I was allowed to feel, let alone admit. We had gotten married at City Hall. I had cried the night before. It had seemed, to me, like a normal response to the situation.

"But otherwise he was going to have to leave."

"That is unfair," Yumiko said. "Not right."

I felt angry at Yumiko for making a judgment right away,

not knowing anything. I wanted to say something, defend Hans, but I did not have the words.

"I could marry the waiter," Yumiko said. "He proposed to me. It was his idea, when I told him my situation. We are sleeping together. But I wouldn't do that to him."

Now, I wished the waiter would come back. I had not properly noticed him. I could not say what was the color of his hair. His eyes. And yet Yumiko had had sex with him.

"Do you want to stay here?" I asked Yumiko.

"Honestly, I would like to be on permanent vacation," she said. "I am reading the great American novels. I have a list in my notebook. I am crossing off the titles, one by one. Big Sur is the best place to hide out from the world."

"Is that what you think I am doing?" I asked her.

"I know I am," she said. "Aren't you?"

She opened the knapsack at her feet.

"What would you like to read?" she said.

She pulled out a novel by Henry Miller, reminding me of my old San Francisco boyfriend. I had always thought his books were wretched, really. Sex and then more sex and then the characters ate dinner, usually at a restaurant in Paris. I shook my head.

"He is big here at Big Sur," Yumiko said.

She had the Fitzgerald from the front desk, *Tender Is the Night*, a book that I loved. "I am reading that one," she said, "so I can't lend it to you."

Yumiko also had Sylvia Plath, *The Bell Jar*, a novel I hadn't read since I was eighteen.

"I'll take the Plath," I said.

"Good choice," Yumiko said.

We sat at the table, quietly reading. It was so nice. The waiter came and refilled our coffee again but I did not notice him until after he was gone. It did not matter. He did not matter. Probably he wasn't good enough for Yumiko, that was usually how it worked. I went back to my book, to reading. It was all so familiar to me, *The Bell Jar*, Esther Greenwood worrying about what lipstick to wear, her suicidal urges. I remembered the sentences as I read them. Suicide, when I was eighteen, had seemed so glamorous, like anorexia.

"I have to go," Yumiko said, suddenly. "But I will see you later."

I nodded.

I had wanted her to be my friend, and now, it seemed, she was my friend. I didn't like how she had judged my marriage but I had gotten past that quickly. Judy would do that, too, say things I did not like. Sometimes, people were allowed to say things that I did not like. I could deal with it. Listen. Explain myself. I wished I had not let myself drift away. Because look what happened. I wondered, anyway, how could I defend Hans. After what had happened. Given the fact that I did not want to read his emails? But I could also say that I loved him, and that was also true. I did love him. I had grown so dependent on Hans. He had worked his way into my life. I was constantly thinking, Hans, he would like it here. He would like this motel, this restaurant overlooking the river, the coffee. The view. The Henry Miller house that was down the road. He would want to go there. He would want to be here with me. We would probably have a nice time together. He would do the driving, drive Judy's red car, and I would like that, not having to drive, but he would also want to listen to music that I didn't like. And I would have to pretend that I didn't hate it. Or plead with him to turn it down. Or negotiate for some Beth Orton.

"La la la," he would say, making fun of my music.

Yumiko left the restaurant.

I watched her go, her black ponytail shining. I found myself envying her pink sweatshirt. I never wore pink, never considered it a color that I could wear, but I realized I could if I wanted to. I realized, in fact, that my kitten T-shirt was pink.

"You are changing," Judy said.

It was one of her more annoying observations and so I ignored her. I could do that. What could she do? She was dead. I finished my coffee. I kept reading. I found myself increasingly irritated with Esther Greenwood, unhappy in New York, miserable despite her fancy internship. I never had a fancy internship. Had I gotten a fancy internship, I would have never been able to afford it anyway. I had always had a job. When I was a child, ten years old, I used to collate binders full of Xeroxed sheets into notebooks, information about my father's stretch wrap machines. I would use the money to buy stuffed animals, elephants usually, they were my favorite animal. I had a collection. But then, my father had an affair with a woman who worked at his company and my mother would not let me work there anymore.

The waiter, Yumiko's ex-boyfriend, or maybe he was still her boyfriend, left the check on my table. For some reason, I had thought that the breakfast came with the cost of the room. It didn't. It was expensive. I paid for Yumiko's pancakes, her coffee, and my eggs and toast, my coffee. I left a generous tip, something I did not always do. I felt bad for the waiter. Because Yumiko was breaking his heart.

I heard her words, echoing in my brain, *Unfair. Not right*, and I thought again of my marriage, of all the meals we had eaten over the course of so many years, all of the meals that I had paid for.

SAT WITH MY FEET IN the river. The water was cold, moving over my feet. I had finished *The Bell Jar* and was rereading Yumiko's copy of *Tender Is the Night*. Two books about suicidal women. I wondered about that. Why they were so popular? I was not suicidal. I felt strangely happy.

Soon, I would stop reading these classic novels written by other people and go back to my own. I had printed out the pages of my manuscript in the office of the motel. Yumiko had opened a new ream of paper for me. She gave me two Pilot pens. She was better than a husband.

"I will miss this job," she said.

Yumiko did not seem surprised when I told her that I finished my novel. She was the first person that I had told.

"I bet it's really good," she said.

"It's just the first draft," I said.

But it was more than a first draft, because the way I wrote, always circling back to the last scene I had written, I had actually rewritten the novel several times over.

"I have a feeling about it," Yumiko said, "and when I have feelings about things, I am always right. I have a powerful sense of intuition."

I didn't believe Yumiko and her powerful sense of intuition. It was also nice to hear.

Judy, for once, didn't have an opinion. Actually, that wasn't true. "You know what I think," she said. Her voice full of disdain.

Actually, I didn't.

I though she would say something positive, but she was also irritated with me, by my needing her to tell me so. It was irritating to me, too, that I required the love and support of a dead person. My graduate program had been full of writers with finished novels. Most of them were no good. I believed I was different. It was arrogant on my part to think that I was any different. But I was also impressed by myself, hidden away at such a beautiful place, working on my book. My job was somehow safely on hold. Diego had been relieved after I wrote him to tell him where I was, that I would be spending the rest of my time in California at Big Sur.

"It was nice," he wrote, "by the way. What happened between us."

It was, sort of.

Or maybe, it wasn't.

There were seventeen emails in my inbox from Hans. Seventeen was an ugly number. A prime number. It made me uncomfortable. It felt unlucky. I did not read them. I did not delete them either. I stared at them, at the subject lines, WHERE ARE YOU, CALL ME, THIS IS GETTING WEIRD, LONELY AND SAD, WHAT THE FUCK, LEAH. I knew they were there, but I did not read them. Once I read these emails, I was lost. I would have to explain. I knew that I would apologize. I knew that whatever I was doing in Big Sur would be over. The emails sat there, in my inbox, in the back of my brain. My mother wrote me, too. I loved my mother. I did not read her email either. Instead, I sent her a postcard.

It seemed funny, my leaving. Judy had died and I had left. But being gone was somehow a helpful reminder of my existence. I was missed by other people. I mattered. I asked Yumiko to take my picture sitting on a bench in the river. Maybe it was the same bench where my mother had her picture taken. I liked to think that it was. There I was, alone, happy in a place where she had once been happy. I wished my mother could be happy more often.

It was idyllic, this spot in California. Quiet. A quiet beauty, different than the majestic cliffs looking down over the Pacific Ocean, only miles away. It was just me and the gentle tinkle twinkle of water, the novel that I was reading, the novel I had written. The emails in the back of my brain. I put down my book and watched a mother duck with her baby ducklings. Four little yellow ducklings. Ridiculously cute. The ducklings were fluffy and round, a pretty soft yellow.

"Hi, little ducks," I said.

And then, from out of nowhere, a hawk swooped down from the sky, taking one of the ridiculously cute yellow ducklings into its mouth and flying away. The mother duck squawked, flapping her wings, water spraying. The three remaining yellow ducklings did not seem to even notice. The fourth duckling was gone. I threw up in my mouth.

YUMIKO KNOCKED ON MY DOOR. I had been asleep, taking a nap. I had been dreaming. She asked if she could borrow my car.

"I don't know," I said.

"You don't know?"

She looked at me, quizzical. A look that said: *Really, you can deny me?*

"She is not that cute," Judy said.

But here, Judy and I had different opinions.

"You don't trust me?" Yumiko asked.

"I don't trust the car," I said.

Yumiko laughed. "That is silly," she said.

It wasn't silly, but I did not want to explain it to her either. She might not believe me. I had difficulty, still, believing that she was the niece of my favorite writer. He would believe me.

"I think the car is possessed," I said, finally.

"You do?"

"With the spirit of my dead friend," I explained. "I am not sure what her intentions were, leaving me this car. I think she loved me, but the car wants me dead. The car is angry."

"So let's go for a drive together," Yumiko said. "You haven't left this place in over a week. It's pretty here but come on. You are in Big Sur."

I rubbed my eyes, gazing at Yumiko in her pink sweatshirt. She never seemed to wear anything else. My dream was slowly coming back to me. I was sitting in the driver's seat of Judy's red car. I was sitting on my hands. The car had known where it wanted to go. We were arguing. I was arguing with a car. The red car was speeding in the left lane, going against the flow of traffic, though I insisted we weren't in England, I was screaming as the car veered, avoiding accidents by insanely small margins, like it was a James Bond movie. I could hear Judy's voice in my dream, calmly telling me to relax, that perhaps we were in England. It was Yumiko's knock at the door that had saved me from dying.

"I don't want to go anywhere," I told Yumiko.

It was true. Since arriving at the River Inn, I had not once desired to go anywhere. I realized, too, that I had been reluctant to get back into Judy's car. It had guided me safely to the motel and that, in itself, seemed fortuitous. I had eaten breakfast every morning with Yumiko, buying her pancakes and coffee. I rewrote my book. Actually, I had finished rewriting it days ago, and Judy was getting impatient with me. But I was not in a hurry. I sat with my feet in the river. I ate wonderful dinners in the restaurant and then I watched bad movies on cable TV in my room. I took baths. I went to sleep early.

"Let's go for a drive," Yumiko said. She put her hands into her pockets and pulled out my car keys.

"You stole them?"

"I have had them for a while," Yumiko said. "They have been waiting for you in the front office. You never noticed."

Still, she had stolen them.

"Where to?" I asked her.

"The ocean," she said. "Where else? Are you coming?"

She knew that I was.

I sat in the passenger seat. It had been over a week since I had been in the car. The windows had been closed. The smell had returned, Judy's perfume. I remembered my journal, which I had put back under the seat. There was no way I was reading that. I felt my leg starting to shake, overwhelmed by Judy's smell. I was afraid that she did not like Yumiko, that she might try something like what had happened with Margaret. I wondered what Judy could possibly have had against Margaret.

"Be careful," I said.

Yumiko turned the keys in the ignition.

The engine roared.

Yumiko let down the windows; she let out a yell. I put on my seat belt. I wondered if Yumiko had her driver's license. I decided not to ask. She was from Japan. How could she? Yumiko looked so young behind the wheel, like a high school girl. I realized this was a very bad idea.

"This is a bad idea," I said out loud.

Yumiko put the car into reverse, backing out onto the highway.

"My uncle says I am a horrible driver," Yumiko said.

"Ha," Judy said, her voice delighted.

And we were off.

In the passenger seat, at least, I could look out the window, look at the view, the breathtaking view that was everywhere, on every turn, every stretch of Highway 1. It was as beautiful as anything I had ever seen. We were way up high, and I gazed out at cliffs overlooking the ocean, at rocky beaches with water that appeared turquoise, as if we were in Hawaii. Wildflowers lined the side of the road, bright purple and pink, yellow and red. I could feel the grin plastered on my face. It was a combination of exultation and fear. Yumiko was driving too fast, but unlike Margaret, she seemed happy and in control.

"I love this car," she yelled. "I love it."

She had to yell, because she was driving so fast. I was glad I could not see the speedometer. I wanted Yumiko to be my friend and she was. I remembered sitting on the steps of Margaret's house with Jonathan Beene. I remembered, again, that this was what it felt like to be happy. His letter had said very little, the address to his loft, his private phone number, the phone number that had not been printed in *The New York Times*.

Yumiko abruptly pulled into a parking lot, the tires screeching in the dirt.

"You are stopping?" I asked.

"Come on," she said.

The view from the parking lot was beyond perfection. The beach was covered with enormous elephant seals sleeping on the sand. How did Yumiko know?

"Thank you," I said to Yumiko. "Thanks for bringing me here."

"You are welcome," Yumiko said. "Eventually you had to leave the motel."

I stepped away from the car, walking over to the guardrail, looking down at the beach, at the seals. They were enormous, so much bigger than sea lions. They lay on top of one another. Looking closer, I saw baby seals, nestled against their mothers.

I closed my eyes.

I felt the sun on my face.

I recognized the sound of my car, pulling out of the parking lot. I opened my eyes and Yumiko was gone. She had told me about the places she wanted to go. San Francisco, Seattle, Portland. She would go to these places. See them before she got back on a plane to Japan. She would drive there in my red car.

"Okay," I said.

"Indeed," Judy said.

I put my hands in my pockets. I had twenty dollars. Two quarters. A lip balm. I looked out at the elephant seals. The baby seals were suckling. I gazed at them, wondering when I had ever seen anything like this before.

The sun was beginning to set, the sky turning brilliant colors. I wished Yumiko well.

T HE WAITER PICKED ME UP.

I had already begun walking back to the motel. It was strangely okay, beautiful, walking along the side of the road as the sun went down, but then it had turned dark, and I was still on the side of the road.

"Now this, actually, is dangerous," Judy said.

A family in a van had pulled over. The seat they offered me was occupied by a bulldog. I told them no. A man in a baseball hat pulled over to offer me a ride. I told him no, too. I would feel stupid, getting raped by a man wearing a hat, when all I had to do was walk a couple more miles. I bent down to tie my shoe and another car idled up beside me. This time it was the pickup truck from the motel. I did not particularly want a ride from the waiter either, but I got in.

"I have been looking for you," he said. "Yumiko called to tell me what she did."

"That was nice of her," I said.

"Nice? She fucking stole your car," the waiter said. "She is a cunt."

The waiter, it turned out, was good-looking. Green eyes. Swoopy hair. He played the guitar, he had a college degree. But I knew, just from the way he said that word, that Yumiko was better off without him. If he had loved her, really loved her, he would never have said that. Even if he was heartbroken until the end of time, he wouldn't have called her that. He would have treasured the *idea* of Yumiko.

Judy sniffed.

"I didn't mean for Yumiko to have the car," she said.

I just hoped that it didn't kill her.

Because, it occurred to me, sitting next to Yumiko's waiter, gazing out the window, that I was glad. Glad she had taken the car. She had done me a favor. Suicide, an accident, it didn't matter. The car had killed Judy. Yumiko had also driven off with my old journal, still tucked away under the seat. I didn't want it. That old me. She had taken her, too.

"She stole your car," Judy said. "My car. She stole my car."

"It's okay," I said.

"What?" the waiter said. "What's okay?"

I smiled. It was the first time I had been caught talking out loud to Judy.

"Everything," I said.

"Bullshit," the waiter said. "Yumiko left. She left me."

The waiter looked unhappy. But he had just called Yumiko a cunt. The hate packed into the word still resonated. It was a horrible word. I thought about Hans, crying, crying when he put me into the taxi.

"I love you," he had said. He had held my hands. He had kissed me. Stroked my hair. He carried my small suitcase down the flight of stairs. "I love you so much, Leah," he said. "So much."

And I got into the taxi.

I rolled down the window.

"It's okay," I had said. Those same words. That's what I

told him. "I'll call you when I land. I'll see you soon. It's just two weeks."

"You will come back?"

"I will come back. I love you," I said. "I love you, too."

I had been lying. They were the words I needed to say, to allow me to get on the plane. I just didn't know it at the time.

AN ENVELOPE WAS WAITING FOR me at my old office, just as I was hoping it would be. Facilities Management. I felt a shiver go through me as I walked through the parking lot. I had it timed just so. My next stop was the airport. Two weeks ago, Diego had bought a plane ticket for two weeks. It had once seemed like such a crazy long amount of time. It had seemed impossible to me, to go away for that long.

Beverly had everything ready.

There was money. I only had to go inside to pick it up. I had to walk by Judy's office to get to Beverly's desk. It was empty. They had not hired a replacement for her yet. Judy was the person, after all, who hired the replacements. I stared at the round table next to her desk, the table where we sat together, where she would sit and knit while we talked. I could see us, sitting there.

I paused in front of her doorway, remembering. I had been so young. Judy had told me that. I had thought I was old. A college graduate.

"Hey, you," Beverly said. "You came back after all."

I wanted to stay there, in the hallway, looking in. I followed Beverly to her cubicle. Judy had always said Beverly was an extremely capable administrative assistant. She still sat in the same cubicle. So close to retirement. She looked younger, I real-

ized, than when I left all those years ago. I found that strange. I
hadn't noticed at the funeral. She caught me staring at her now.

"I started dyeing my hair," Beverly said.

"It looks good," I said.

"You keep in touch." Beverly touched my shoulder. It was
as if I was already gone, her attention turning back to her computer, the work she had to do. Now that I had stepped away
from Judy's office, I wanted to get the hell out of there anyway.
"It was a treat to see you," she said. "Come back soon."

"You'll be here." It came out before I could stop myself. It
was not a kind thing to say. Judy hooted.

"Only five more years before my pension."

Five years. That seemed in the realm of possible. I found
myself hoping that Beverly was happy. That secretly she enjoyed
hating her job. That she did not really hate it as much as she
had claimed, for all those years.

"No, she hates it," Judy said.

"Thank you, again," I told Beverly.

It was a manila envelope with my name written on it. Inside,
the envelope there was another envelope. A check. It was the
money Judy had written about. It was not a massive amount.
But it was enough for a while. To rent a new apartment, to
pay for a security deposit, to live for one month or maybe two.

"Until you sell your novel," Judy said.

I winced.

"You think you are going to jinx yourself?" Judy said.
"That's ridiculous."

There was one more envelope still, the invitation to
her niece's bat mitzvah. I had forgotten, again, about the
bat mitzvah. The invitation was printed on cream-colored

paper, engraved, addressed to Judy. She had known she would never go.

The bat mitzvah was the next day in a suburb of Philadelphia. There was no way I could make it. I was in San Francisco. My flight that night was back to New York. I had to go home. I had to go back, even if I did not want to. I had said that I was going back. I had said it. And then, I thought about the logistics. The bat mitzvah. Judy's last wish. I did the math, calculating the ins and outs of the trip. Of course, I could make it. I could arrive just in time.

"Got you," Judy said.

I shrugged.

It was time for me to go.

I started walking.

"I almost forgot," Beverly called, chasing after me. She handed me a small canvas, the size of a paperback book. It was a painting. The painting Judy had left for me. Wildflowers. They were like the flowers I had seen on the side of the road, along Highway 1. The beautiful wildflowers. Purple and pink, red and orange and yellow.

"This is so beautiful," I said.

I held the painting to my chest.

"Thank you," Judy said. "My honey."

IEGO DROVE ME TO THE airport.

I wondered what that had been, the two of us, back in his apartment. I had been drunk. But he wasn't. Or maybe he was. I didn't have a crush on him anymore and somehow that made me sad. Diego apologized for not parking the car, but he had a meeting he had to get back for. He dropped me off at the departure gate. It was an uneventful drive. We did not talk. I felt grateful for his sleek but sensible silver car. It was as if I had passed some kind of test, not letting the red car kill me. And I would be okay.

"Keep in touch, okay?" Diego said.

This, it seemed to me, was the thing that you said to someone you never expected to see again. He was still so ridiculously cute. Diego. He still worked in my old office. He made a lot of money. I had gotten away.

"I will," I told Diego. "And thank you."

I kissed him on the lips.

It was what I wanted to do.

TOOK THE AIR TRAIN TO the subway to Penn Station.

I waited half an hour and then boarded Amtrak to Philadelphia. I ran across the station at Thirtieth Street, bought my ticket, and then waited another six minutes, taking the commuter train to the suburb where Judy's sister lived. Probably, I should have rented a car, but I didn't want to drive again.

Not for a while.

The town was not far from Haverford. The train, in fact, passed the Haverford station. I nodded when the conductor called out its name, almost as if to pay my respects.

From the window, I could see the back of the Wawa, the very same Wawa that was across the street from the duck pond where I used to go after class, when it all felt like too much. Where I had gone just to look at the ducks. I knew it was there, the duck pond, even if I couldn't see it.

I had never gone back.

The conductor called my station and I got off the train. I caught a taxi and told the driver the name of the synagogue. In the backseat, I brushed my hair. I put on lipstick. I thought about putting on mascara but decided not to bother. I was fine. I was wearing my black funeral dress.

"You look nice," the taxi driver said.

I patted my bags. I had my small carry-on bag. I had my backpack. I had my laptop computer. I had Judy's painting. I held it carefully. The bat mitzvah had already started when I arrived.

I slipped into the back row. I did not know anyone there. I did not understand the Hebrew being spoken from the stage. I had not been in a synagogue since I was thirteen years old, for my best friend's bat mitzvah. I tried to remember the last time I had been in a church. It had been in Austria, the funeral for Hans's grandmother. I had looked around furtively, staring at all of the old people filling the pews. They had been alive during the Holocaust.

I looked up at the teenage girl standing on the stage, standing behind the podium. She was also wearing a sleeveless black dress, a simple Audrey Hepburn dress very much like mine. She was lovely. The door had squeaked when I entered the room and everyone turned around to look at me, late.

The girl, Judy's niece, had also looked at me, a question in her glance. She had no idea who I was. She had messed up her verse, but then she took a breath and continued. I had not ruined her rite of passage. She was fine.

She looked just like Judy.

"Just look at her," Judy said.

I did. I looked at her. I looked. Judy's niece? Her daughter? Could that have been her daughter? I wondered what I would say to her. I could not remember her name, written on the invitation. I wondered what I would say to her. What I would tell her about Judy and how she died. And how she had lived. I wondered where I would live next. I would not go home. I wondered what kind of food would be served at the reception. I was hungry.

ACKNOWLEDGMENTS

Thanks to Liveright/Norton for making this book possible: Katie Adams, Cordelia Calvert, and Peter Miller, I am grateful for everything that you do.

Thanks to Alex Glass, my smart and loyal agent, for sticking by me.

Thanks to my smart and loyal friends and family, who have also stuck by me (in alphabetical order): Sarah Bardin, Lauren Cerand, Ann Dermansky, Ira Dermansky, Julie Dermansky, Michael Dermansky, Nina Dermansky Fauth, Melissa Johnson, Heather Paxson, Stefan Helmreich, Shelley Salamensky, Talya Shomron, Lizzie Skurnick, Adina Taubman, and Sondra Wolfer.